# Necromancer's Garden

Shauna McGuiness

This book is a work of fiction. Any references to historical events, real people, or real locales are used fictitiously. Other names, characters, places, and incidents are the product of the author's imagination, and any resemblance to actual events or locales or persons, living or dead, is entirely coincidental.

Printed by Kindle Direct Publishing, An Amazon.com Company
Available from Amazon.com and other online stores
Available on Kindle and other devices

ISBN: 9798526722131

"…I am fearfully and wonderfully made…"
**Psalm 139:14**

I cy wet covered us, shocking us both. She gripped my arm, her fingernails digging into my nearly numb skin. The current was powerful and it pulled me toward the bridge. I could see men standing there now, guarding the gate.

Kicking with all the strength I could muster, I dragged my precious cargo along, coming up every few seconds so we could breathe. After what seemed like hours in the frigid water, my feet found purchase in the claylike surface. Standing on the bank, we tried to catch our breath.

"See those men over there?" I asked her, pointing in the direction of the bridge. My hand shook vigorously. "They think they're waiting for us, so stay down. We're going to head in the other direction."

She nodded, cheeks quivering with cold.

Looping my bag around my shoulder, I pulled my partner in crime toward a lone, thick pine tree, giving us a moment to breathe.

1

"When I say, 'Go,' I want you to run as fast as you can. If we can get a bit further before they see us, we might be able to make it. Once we get to the city's border, we'll be safe."

Looking up at me with those huge eyes, hair dripping, shivering in the breeze, I wondered why I hadn't gotten her out sooner. All those years I watched her suffer humiliation and isolation. I knew she had family on The Outside, yet I'd done nothing to reunite them.

Now was my chance. I would not fail.

"Okay," I warned her. "Go!"

# SHAR'N

My mother is alive in my dreams. Peering into her face feels like seeing a future image of myself. Black hair hangs in waves around her pale skin and eyes the shape of large almonds look on me fondly, both of which look like my own. My eyes are blue, but hers are a green so light that they almost appear yellow, like an intelligent, wary wolf's. In my dreams I save her life. Everyone thinks I am a hero; they bake cakes with my name written in white sugary frosting and sing songs with the tale of my victory in the chorus. They all want to have a place by my side.

When I wake, I know I'm not a hero. No one wants to be near me. *Because I killed my mother.*

Did you know that there are fifteen dead mothers per 100,000 live babies each year? I'm willing to bet that I am the only one out of the fifteen babies in the year I was born who had the ability to bring her mother back to life. And I failed.

In a field of flowers, I am a bush. Literally. The females all have names like Rose, Daisy, and Bluebell. I am called Shar'n, short for "Rose of Sharon." My name is derived from a shrub, while those around me are solidly flowers. *Rose of Sharon.* Close enough to sound like another flower, but definitely a bush.

It is Harvest week, so every female in our community is responsible for plucking as many presentable flowers as she can. That's how we make our money. The men bring the flowers to the Outsiders who buy them for flower shops, hotel and restaurant table arrangements, and funeral homes. The men plant and we harvest, doing the work that leaves us sweaty and exhausted. Standing in a long line, each in our own row, we hold metal shears, trying earnestly not to bend the blooms that we clip as we go. The sun shines hot on our backs as the scent of thousands of flowers nearly overwhelms us, sickly sweet in the warm spring air. So thick that it is almost tangible, the combination of smells drapes our hunched bodies, suffocating us. My gloves make it hard to feel the stems, and some slip as I continue down the row, but I dare not stop to pick them up. Any slowing draws the attention of the Field Master.

No one will work in my proximity, but it is just as well. I can't abide being close to anybody anyway. Except for Peter. He's male, so he doesn't have to participate in The Harvest.

Expediently moving along my assigned line of flowers, I fill my bucket, carefully avoiding the ones that didn't survive this time. Those ones return to the soil, the fallen helping to feed the next round of blooms. If I could take off my gloves, I could bring the brown, dried-out blossoms back, breathing life into the delicate petals. The People would kill me for sure, though, if I did that.

They all hate me because I terrify them.

They all hate me because I'm the Necromancer.

# COUSINS

# SHAR'N

W hen everyone thought I was normal, they used to smile and hug and let me sit on their laps. I recall walking into neighbors' houses without knocking, being handed cool lemonade and warm, fresh cookies. Nobody handed me cool beverages or sweets anymore.

Life changed for the better when I met Peter. He also had popularity issues, though he wasn't hated half as much as I was. Always ill with something or other, Peter was skinny and tall with hair that refused to lay down. He was like an underfed scarecrow with allergies and eczema. Peter was the only one who wasn't daunted by the thing I could do. He thought it amazing and watched me do it time and again.

It was easy to sneak away when everyone convinced themselves you weren't there. After school, once my chores were completed, Peter and I liked to sit in the grey shadow of the abandoned barn. We talked about books we'd read and gossip we'd heard. When you're invisible, as we were, people sometimes forgot to watch what they were saying.

Technically, I was not allowed to read anything that hadn't been assigned in class. Girls were forbidden from reading non-instructional literature, but I read with a voraciousness that scared me sometimes. The characters in books were my friends, my family. My father had a low bookshelf in his room packed with hundreds of books of all subjects and lengths. The first one I dared to borrow was *20,000 Leagues Under the Sea*. I couldn't believe how alive words could be, twisting and breathing life into the story. After that I was unstoppable. I swallowed every whole book you can imagine. Cat sat on my lap while I read, and there was no fear we'd be discovered since no one dared visit my little room in the back of the house.

Crime novels, classics, mysteries, thrillers. Obviously Father was a reader, too. It was a shame I could never have revealed I'd read all the same stories that he had. We could have been quite a book club, he and I. Instead, I'd sneak into his room, stealthily replacing one book and taking another, an unlikely vandal of the literary variety. His frequent visits with the Outsiders, past the boundary, allowed him to visit bookstores. With every trip he replenished his collection, adding new best sellers to the shelf. *What must it feel like, standing in the middle of a shop full of books?* Walls covered from floor to ceiling in papered treasure. I tried to imagine such a beautiful thing. How it must smell...paper and adhesive and *freedom*.

Words. Words to me were more delicious than the most exquisite bite of chocolate. I gobbled them as if I were starving, but I never became too full.

Peter liked to read, also, but he was allowed to do it, so it wasn't the same. I often wondered what the men thought they were trying to do, keeping us from reading. Did they think they were protecting us? Most likely, they were protecting *themselves* from the danger of knowledgeable females.

Through my beloved hobby, I learned that the way we lived was very unusual. The first time I read about a female doctor, I was thoroughly shocked. Women were out there being lawyers, doctors, teachers—important people. They went to school, they learned. They did more than communally raise children, share a husband, and snip countless flowers. I supposed that sort of information could be dangerous.

Females in our community who were caught reading books were punished, and the patriarch of the family got to decide how it was done. I had no clue what kind of punishment my father would choose, but he was a fan of the switch, so I was reasonably sure a whipping would commence following the discovery of what I'd been doing for years. I halfway thought it would still be worth it. This never happened during my lifetime, which led me to believe I might possibly be the only female in my community who had developed a taste for forbidden literature.

The wives pretended that I didn't exist, and they trained my siblings to do the same. Not an easy thing to do when all twenty-four of us lived in a five-bedroom house.

The only truly wonderful thing about being a pariah is that I had my own living space. There was one bedroom for the seven girls, one for the eight boys, a room for the wives, one for my father, and one for me. All those bodies squeezed into rows of bunk beds, but not the wives; their narrow beds line the room like matches in a box. Father's room was the largest and had a connected bath. The rest of the occupants had to wait for the other remaining bathroom in the house. The scarcity of tubs made a bathing schedule necessary. The bathing schedule made things a little uncomfortable for those who needed the bathroom for other reasons.

The wives turned around and went in the other direction if we ended up in the hall together, and the children were taught to avert their eyes if we should come face to face. When I was very small, it hurt to be so completely rejected. I knew why they all shunned me, but the knowing did nothing to soothe my loneliness. Teachers at school always placed my desk at the back of the room, and it was an unspoken, unwritten rule that I was not allowed to touch the jump ropes or the scuffed red rubber balls that the other students used for four-square. I sat at my own lunch table, not sharing cookies or trading sandwiches like all the other children did with smiles and giggles—and ungloved hands.

Those who fed and diapered me when I was a baby were a mystery. This was before my gift was discovered, and I sometimes imagined that someone—maybe more than just one someone—may have loved me, the helpless infant without a mother. There were no wives then because my mother had been the only one that my father wanted. When she was gone, he began to marry. And marry. Perhaps he was trying to find a woman who could fill the vacancy that my mother created when she left this world. With each new bride, Father's mood became lighter, but it never lasted long. It was as though he believed he found someone who could make him feel again. He was *sure this time*. But then the new woman would disappoint in some way. She wouldn't be as graceful or as beautiful as my mother. She would say the wrong things or cook the wrong food.

My grandmother must have taken care of me. My father was the youngest of eight born by her. Grandmother never liked my mother, and those feelings extended to me, even before she knew about my gift. Grandmother died when I was six, long after she already made it known that I was not welcome anywhere near her.

Peter was the only person on this earth who reminded me I was a solid, breathing human being. When I was with him I could remove my gloves. They were made of soft, tan leather and I supposed my father and his wives liked to pretend they almost looked like skin. Like unafflicted hands. They were hot and tight and made picking up small items almost impossible. Good luck to me if I ever dropped a flat button on the ground.

The fingers beneath appeared unremarkable. Slim, paler than the attached arms, tipped with smooth fingernails. It's what they we capable of doing that made them the number-one top feared pair of appendages on our little corner of the planet. When those average looking fingers touched something that had breathed its last breath, they reeled life right back in. Insects, plants, animals—I'd done it. I never experimented on a human being, but I was irrevocably certain that it would work. I just didn't know if there would be some sort of consequence.

Peter brought me a butterfly. Nestled in the creases of his palm were large, flat wings. Bright orange and lovely, but unmoving.

The insect was obviously dead.

"Will you?" he asked, breathless with excitement, a light whistle of asthma daring to surface.

I didn't answer. Instead, I cupped my hands together and accepted the still creature.

I felt nothing at first. But then a buzz filled my fingertips, crawling toward my first knuckles, creeping toward my wrists. Soon, I couldn't feel my hands at all. I know it sounds impossible, but I heard the butterfly take a sharp, jagged breath. She flipped onto her belly, drowsily, wings quivering.

Peter dared not make a sound.

"Fly away," I whispered.

And she did.

# CHRYS

I couldn't believe that girl was such a loser-ass bitch. I *told* her I liked Brendan. I made her SWEAR she wouldn't tell anyone. By lunchtime, she'd taken a pic of him and posted it on her Insta, writing on his forehead in purple squiggly letters. His title? "Chrys's Crush." Thanks a lot Lauren!

*Just wait till I figure out how to get back at her.* She peed the bed 'till fifth grade, but that just didn't seem good enough to get her back. I just needed a little time. I'd dig up something really good.

Damn, I wish I didn't always have so much freakin' homework. I'd rather watch TV or roleplay online. Anything other than do that history crap. My mom would kill me if I didn't get on the assistant principal's honor roll, at least, so I had to try.

My mom was pretty tight most of the time. She listened to cool music and had a hot pink streak in her hair that showed when she pulled it into a ponytail. She let me have friends over and answered any questions that I had, even if they were really embarrassing. I guess she was a keeper. She worked all the time, because she had, like, three different jobs: tutor, parent newsletter editor for a preschool, and writer. I knew she wished she could just write, but there were bills to be paid, and let's face it, I was too lazy to do anything about that yet. Anyway, Mom said my job was to do well in school. So, I guessed I'd better make some sort of attempt at it.

We were escapees. I didn't remember anything about actually *being* an escapee, but it sounded cool, so I told people about it every chance I got. My mom joined a cult when she was a little older than me. They didn't call themselves a cult, but it sure sounded like one when she was up to talking about it, which really wasn't all that often. She said to call them "a religious community" and that they believed themselves to be working under the word of God, but somewhere along the line something got seriously screwy. For example, Mom was eighteen when she got married. And my dear ol' Dad? He had two other wives at the time. And he was sixty-four. *Sixty-four?* Ewwwww. I didn't remember him, and I was sort of glad.

They called themselves The People, like there was some sort of doubt about their species, like maybe they were actually animals for a while, but then became human, or something. They believed many wives were needed to bring many children into the world. Many children who would spread the word. *The word about what? How to marry teenagers to old dudes?* Sounded pretty creepy to me.

Mom said she joined The People's Land because her sister joined first. My Aunt Lily fell in love with some guy she met when he was in town selling flowers. *True Love,* she said. They had a baby, but my aunt didn't survive. My mother decided, kinda too late, that she had only joined to be with her sis, but my father wouldn't hear it. Mom was trapped.

Mom won't say much about this time. She only said that she couldn't stay chained up while other women raised her only child. Actually, she said "other hoes raised my child." It seemed so...unlike her. My mom was actually pretty classy, pink hair and all.

Anyway, we left when I was two. Mom didn't have any money, but she knew someone on The Outside who helped her along until she could help herself. Because Mom was super smart it didn't take long for her to figure out how to support the two of us, but we were still close to Grammy Esther, who lived in the apartment next door and cooked us dinner more often than not. Grammy Esther was an escapee, too, but of another kind. She still had the number tattooed on her forearm to prove it. Mom says Grammy's time was harder than ours. Millions were killed, including Grammy's family, by a monster, named Hitler. He was a psycho with a weird mustache, but he totally got people to listen to him, anyway.

Mom only lost her sister. But it was enough.

So, maybe I should keep ignoring stupid rumors and posts on Tumblr and Insta by stupid people who annoyed me. The struggles of those around me reminded me of how lame my little problems were.

I had a cousin who still lived where I used to. Mom said we looked alike, with the same eyes.

I didn't even know her name, but I decided I needed her help.

Mom spent a ton of time talking about how glad she was to have gotten us out. All I could think about was finding a way to get back in.

# SHAR'N

I t had been a very strange day.
I got a package.

I'd never received anything in the mail before, as far as I could remember. No one wanted anything to do with me, so any sort of special communication was unheard of. Still, my teacher, Mr. Adams, called my name after attendance and handed it to me, carefully extending the envelope away from his body.

Mr. Adams was supposed to be a great Christian, as all our teachers were required to be. He taught us about God with a pious face and steepled hands, reminding us daily of our role as females in our community.

He was terrified of me.

I was much too embarrassed to act interested, or to actually shred the top open on the yellow envelope. But I was very curious. The package seemed to sing a siren's song, calling to me. I tucked it under my notebook, but it was just a tiny bit larger. The sharp corners seemed to taunt me, seemed to say, "Aren't you going to open me yet?" The rest of the class was doing a poor job of hiding their own curiosity, but of course no one would ask me about it. They tried their best to act as though it didn't exist. Just as they acted like I didn't exist.

At lunchtime, Peter sat next to me and unwrapped his lunch: leftover roasted chicken, soda bread, and an apple.

"Well?" he asked.

"Well, what?" I refused to meet his stare.

"Are you going to open it?" Peeling a strip of chicken away from the bone, he popped it in his mouth and chewed, still looking at me.

"How did you know?" He had been in the boys' upper grades classroom all morning.

"Are you kidding? Biggest news in ages! Must be hard for them to pretend you're not around when that package is all anyone can talk about." He laughed wryly. "So, are you? Going to open it, I mean."

"Not here. I don't know why, but I just... Not here."

"The barn, after school?" he asked, hopefully. He tugged at his suspenders, like he always did when he was nervous. Peter also tended to pull on the brim of his straw hat, both obvious "tells."

I nodded. The thought of the hardboiled egg in my cloth lunch bag made me feel nauseous. I half-heartedly bit the end of a carrot and struggled to swallow it.

The yellow envelope tried to burn its way out of my satchel. The bag leaned against my leg, and I swear it felt warm.

Sitting in a shady corner away from the rest of the population, we watched the other students play. The younger ones kicked the balls around the yard or played on the monkey bars. The teenagers walked in circles around the small field, trading secrets. I bet I could beat any secret that's ever been divulged along that short trail.

Just before the bell rang, I leaned into Peter's ear and whispered, "Are you still reading *The Shining*?"

He nodded and whispered back, "It's kind of scaring me a little. I'll keep reading, though, if you will."

A whole section of Father's library was dedicated to Stephen King. At first the books frightened me. When I got through *Carrie*, and then *Firestarter*, I began to fantasize that there could be other people who could do things like I could. I realized the books were just works of fiction, but the ideas must have come from *somewhere*...

"I'll keep reading. It scares me, too, but I have to find out what happens. I hope they all get away from that hotel."

Collecting our bags, we dusted off our rear ends— mine covered by a long, rough brown skirt, his by black trousers a little too short for his lanky frame—and headed back to our gender-separated classes.

# CHRYS

M om had been sick for a while. She acted like she was fine. She still went to work, laughed at my jokes, and asked about my day.

New crow's feet grew around her eyes, and her shoulders became narrower. She swore she felt okay, but I didn't believe her.

It was the cancer. It had come back.

What cruel irony would have my mother harvesting flowers for hours, days, weeks—without any sort of protection from the sun—and escaping from that freak-o place, but taking a crappy passenger with her? Also freakin' lame was the fact that she wasn't even there for that long. Three years was enough to lay the groundwork for all sorts of nasty to start growing. People all over the world lathered up with baby oil and baked intentionally, and all they got was a leathery chest. Skin cancer sucked.

They removed it all from her face, leaving faint scars, which look pretty cool, really. One over her left eyebrow looked passably like an anarchy symbol. *Rock 'n' Roll, Mama!*

We always knew it might spread. She wasn't talking, but I was pretty sure I got it figured out. And I figured something else out, too. I knew how to save her.

My mother used to tell me all kinds of stories about her sister, and the times that they'd had growing up. Their first shared cigarette (*don't even think about it*, she always said). First boyfriends (*think about it, but not too much*, she always said). They were "Irish twins" born only eleven months apart. They could have been real twins, for the connection they felt to one another. Their mom, my grandmother, died from breast cancer when the girls were fourteen, and their father remarried a woman who couldn't stand them. Mom says they even caught their stepmother, Carole, trying to poison them with weed killer. She was adding a pinch to her spaghetti sauce just as my mom entered the kitchen. Their father had been out of town on a business trip at the time, and he didn't believe a word of their accusation when he got back. Never mind that Lily had been having stomach problems for months and Mom had permanent dark circles under her eyes. Things got so bad that they ran away the week after my mom graduated from high school. The girls traveled by bus, as far as their money would reach, landing in my hometown. Within days, my Aunt Lily got a waitressing job, and Mom ended up as a drugstore cashier. They talked to my grandfather a few times before he died from a heart attack, but he never forgave them for "being mean to Carole."

My Aunt Lily fell in love the moment she met Joseph. They married quickly, and Mom had to follow, because she was afraid Lily would never come back to see her. They didn't have phones at The People's Land, either. Mom was worried. She followed her sister and didn't look back.

A rough pregnancy brought them closer than ever. I had already been born, and so Mom was the wiser one. The birth of my cousin killed Lily. It devastated my mother, and also Joseph. Mom tried to help him with the baby. She said it was like having twins since we were so close in age. She even nursed the other baby, which really wigged me out, but *whatever*. She was a better person than I was.

When my cousin and I were two, Mom hit the road. She said the place was too freaky to stay without her sister. Guilt has plagued her since the day we escaped because she believed she should have taken my cousin, too. Sometimes, when she'd had a little too much wine, she talked about the child.

From early on she knew something was very special about the baby. She was able to do things other people couldn't do. Mom only saw it happen a couple of times, but that was enough. That was the reason she stayed so long, actually. Worry about what might happen if the child's secret was discovered held her as surely as heavy chains. As time passed, the child's strange talent seemed to go unnoticed.

So, we left.

*Oh. My. God. If Lauren doesn't stop texting me, I am going to kill her.* If her mom would have bought her a freakin' iPhone like everyone else on the planet, her texts wouldn't have cost me money. FIVE texts in two minutes. Couldn't she have just written one long one, or something? Or picked up the damn phone? Her stupid obsession with Steven Ku was costing me some serious dough.

"Lauren," I shouted after she picked up her end, "stop texting me, you big nerd! Every text costs me, like, twenty cents. That last round was a whole dollar. That's like, a Coke, or something."

"Sorry, Chrys, I'm just excited. He asked me to the dance!" she squealed.

I pulled the phone away from my ear before she could bust my eardrum, then I hung up on her. Maybe I should have signed into Tumblr and blasted the world about *her* crush.

See how *she* felt about it.

# SHAR'N

I n addition to The Harvest, which took place every other
week, each female over the age of ten was required to
have two jobs at home. We dutifully went about finishing
our chores after school and during Harvest weeks we were
still expected to do our jobs, working in the dark once we'd
returned home.

Most of my half-sisters were in charge of doing dishes,
whacking the rugs out in the yard, and finding things in our
little garden to add to dinner. The one closest to my age,
Blonde Lilac, was almost thirteen. She had recently been
allowed to begin doing some of the cooking. I'm sure you
can imagine no one ever let me near their food. I was not
quite sure what they were so frightened of. It wasn't as
though a pork chop would reanimate under my touch.

One of my duties was to empty all the trash from the
house when necessary. Some of it went into the garden in
the form of compost. Some went to a pig trough that we
shared with the community. The rest was burned.

I was also in charge of the underclothes.

I didn't know of any other family within The People's Land—sounded like a strange amusement park, didn't it? Or a foreign translation of some other title? —who separated their underthings from the rest of the clothes, so I was pretty sure that it was meant to be a snub toward me. Peter and I had mulled it over countless times. Who came up with the idea? Did they laugh at me behind their uncovered hands? Or had they become so accustomed to me washing their dainties that they no longer cared, tossing them in a separate hamper for me to deal with on Wednesdays? It was a big wicker hamper with "Rose of Sharon" painted in red on the side in drippy paint.

The one thing that I enjoyed about those days was that I could remove my gloves while doing laundry. No life could be risen from cloth diapers, soiled underpants, bloomers or camisoles. I stretched my fingers and moved them as if I were playing a piano. The freedom made me content, if only for a second. Cat stopped by for a quick hello and I gave him a good scratch with my uncovered hands. How warm and soft his fur was when not buffered by tight leather coverings.

A fire pit was created just for me so that I could boil water without stepping into the kitchen. The cauldron, much like the one I imagined the witches in Macbeth used, hung above the pit. Garbage that could be safely burned from our house was deposited there, by me, all week. *Double, double toil and trouble; fire burn, and cauldron bubble*, indeed. A thick, tall club-like stick sat in the empty tub until I was ready to fill and *stir, stir, stir*. Boiling away the multitudes of filth excreted by people who would rather I not be alive, adding potent lye to the concoction. An oddish stew, to say the least.

Don't mistake this as a simple job. Recall that there were over twenty of us, and there are seven days of the week. Even those with little skill in mathematics can surmise how very large the pile of intimate underthings would grow.

I washed them and hung them to dry, returning a couple of hours later to sort them using the names sewn into the waistbands. The diapers all went into one basket, to surround the bellies of the many still wearing them in the family. The clothes took quite a lot longer to dry on Harvest Wednesdays, when the sun had already disappeared. The moon didn't make speedy work of readying things for removal from the line. On those days, I found myself rising at a ridiculously early hour to pull everything down and sort it after hanging for the night. I was to leave them on the porch in each person's basket. The baskets would then disappear into the house. It seemed to all inside that the Underclothes Fairy had come and gone, just like always.

The Underclothes Fairy. That was my lot in life.

Once everything was strung up across the back of the house with wooden clothespins, I returned my gloves to each hand, snatched up the yellow envelope, and headed for the barn. I could barely wait to meet Peter so we could see what the envelope held within.

# CHRYS

S o, I didn't even know my cousin's name. My mom wouldn't tell me. She said it hurt too much to think about the baby she left behind. I really wanted to get in touch with her, though, so I was going to have to figure out how to get a message to her.

I looked through the drawer where Mom kept all her writing supplies. She used to send submissions to magazines using big, golden-yellow envelopes. She mostly used email these days, but there is still a fat stack of envelopes left. They looked all official, so I thought I'd use one of those to start.

From what I knew, The People's Land—sounded like some seriously messed up amusement park or something— peeps were totally old-fashioned, so I didn't want to send anything that looked too modern, like a mailing label. I'd only seen guys in town, but they looked kind of Amish or something. They all wore black pants and vests with homemade-looking white shirts. The shirts didn't have collars, and the outfits reminded me of a production of *The Crucible* my school did last fall. I wasn't in it, but Lauren was. She didn't have any lines, just did a lot of shrieking and gasping. It was all right.

Anyway, the clothes were weird, and they were topped off with straw hats. But I had to admit that some of the guys were kind of hot. I mean, put 'em in some skinny jeans and a hoodie, and Lauren might have gotten over Steven Ku pretty fast.

I wrote a letter using the formatting that I barely remember from elementary school. Address on the left, date on the right, *yada, yada, yada*. Who sent letters anymore, anyway? Well, it looked like I did.

I didn't dare ask Mom for the address, so I did the best I could. My cousin would be in the same grade as me, if they did things like we did, and I knew her father's name. Those were my only clues.

I swear I did the best I could.

## SHAR'N

P eter wasn't waiting for me.
Sitting in the shade of the barn, I placed the letter
across my palms, reading what was written on the front in
large scrolling cursive for the hundredth time, it seemed.

*Daughter of Joseph*
*11th Grade*
*The People's Land*

Ninth through eleventh grades were taught together if
you were female, and my father was the only Joseph with a
daughter at the high school level. The boys went to separate
classes, and we only saw them at recess. While we studied
books about flowers, recited passages from the Bible, and
learned how to read recipes, the boys did math, history,
science. They also continued through the twelfth grade
unless they turned eighteen first. If that happened, they
could choose to finish out the year or be finished with

school altogether. Once they graduated from twelfth grade, the boys became part of the flower delivery process. Most of the girls were married by the time eleventh grade rolled around, so there was no need for them to continue. I should have said "us." *There was no need for "us" to continue.* I wasn't planning to find myself in that situation, however, because who would marry me?

Father was known as Dark Joseph. He had full black hair, a black beard, thick black eyebrows, and dark, dark eyes. I'm sure he thought his nickname was derived from his appearance, but it came from somewhere deeper. I couldn't remember the last time I saw him smile. A serious, brooding man, he provided for his family and brought his wives to his bedroom in rotation, but he rarely spoke to anyone. Working as a bookkeeper for our export business served him well. Numbers never struggled for awkward, polite conversation.

Whatever was inside my mysterious delivery was very light. When I held it up to my face and blew air on to it, the envelope shifted across my palms, ever so slightly. I almost decided to open it by myself when Peter came bounding around the corner, landing breathless at my side in a tangle of limbs.

"Sorry." It was all he had to say. I knew that he had been subjected to another one of his father's daily lectures. Every day after Peter and his seven school-age siblings returned from school, the patriarch of their family questioned how Godly and studious they had behaved throughout the school day. Lemuel was a skilled berater and found creative ways to nag his brood about their unavoidable trip to Hell. The name Lemuel Loquacious fit him very well (there were three Lemuels among us; one was Peter's father, one was his brother, and one was his grandfather). The chronically progeny-disappointed man loved to hear himself talk, doing so with great energy and to the humiliation of others.

As I slid my pointer finger under the section of flap not adhered together, Peter leaned against me. I could feel him breathing, his chest lifting in anticipation. He smelled like grass, fresh air and boy.

The ripping sound the paper made seemed so much louder than it should have been. It was a delicious, crisp sound. A single sheet of flat white paper slipped out like it had been anticipating its release.

An address from The Outside was scrawled at the top left corner. The date from two days ago was at the right.

*Hello,*

*I wish I knew what to call you, but I don't know your name. What I do know is that we are related. We're cousins. My mother is your aunt. Her sister was your mother. I've always wondered about you and wished that we could meet.*

*Although I know meeting you is probably not a possibility, I was wondering if you could help me? When Mom left, she left religion, too. I'm curious about so many things! I thought maybe we could* [correspond had twice been spelled incorrectly, erased well, but not quite well enough] *write to each other? I have a desire to know God. I just don't know where to find him.*

*Please write back.*

*Sincerely*
*Chrys Perkins*

"Woah," breathed Peter.

"She wants a religious tutor?" I wondered.

"Looks like it," Peter smiled. "You're not a bad one for the job, you know."

"How did she know about me? I didn't know I had a cousin...on The Outside."

"Writing her back would be a good way to find out, don't you think?"

"I think I'd like to do it, Peter! I think I will! Maybe I can ask her all about living out there? I wonder if it's just like in books, or if it–"

"Slow down, tiger." Peter took my shoulders and turned me toward his concerned face. "Be careful, *Fleur.* Don't make anyone mad. They hate you enough as it is. Don't give them any excuses to make things any worse than they have to be."

"Why did you call me that?" I looked away, not sure what to make of it.

"Because I'm serious. *And it's your real name.* And...I want you to know that I care for you and I meant what I said." He forced my chin so that I had to meet his eyes once again.

"Yes. Yes, okay." Scooting for some distance, I said, "Better get back. It's time to sort the laundry." I wanted to ponder the letter in the private, quiet corridors of my mind.

"Be careful," Peter warned again, smoothing his hair then returning his hat to his head. "I mean it."

Tucking the precious letter under my arm, I ran to finish my chore.

# CHRYS

It shouldn't be a big deal, right? I mean, it was just a stupid letter. No one cared that I wrote a note to my cousin.

*Ugh. I feel so guilty!*

If I told my mom, it would totally freak her out, but I had to tell *someone*. I kept myself from telling Lauren all day because she had such a big mouth. She would have told Sadie and Jackie and Joey and the whole campus—before lunch!

Every fingernail was gone. Every single damn one chewed to little ragged nubs that kept catching on my rayon skirt. There was even a little run in the front now. I was afraid to pull it because it might have made a hole, and of course it was my favorite.

I tried to get into the book that I was reading for English, *The Grapes of Wrath*, but it was so sad. And boring. And who has a name like Joad, anyway? My foot bounced and bounced until I kicked over my Diet Sprite and had to run for the paper towels.

*Grammy Esther will listen,* I thought. And she did.

Grammy had a way of listening that made you think that she wasn't. She never made eye contact while you talked, and always had this weird little smile on her face. You'd kind of feel like she'd tuned you out completely, but then she'd offer the most amazing advice. Stuff you never would have thought of on your own.

A wide, wrinkled smile welcomed me into her apartment, which was across the hall from ours. Her iPad Mini was propped up on the smallish, carefully polished coffee table. Grammy Esther's hands were gnarled with arthritis, but she really loved to play solitaire, so Mom and I bought her the little tablet for her birthday (then I fell in love with it and asked for one for my birthday). Poking at a screen was easier for her than shuffling cards.

She sat at one end of her doily-covered couch, stockinged legs crossed at the ankle. At the other end I blustered and talked. It sounded like I was trying to convince *myself* that it was no big deal. *No one was hurt. They were just words.*

"Words can be *very* painful," Grammy said, once she finally looked at me.

"Well, crap. It's already too late." I sighed and picked at the run in my skirt.

"What's done is done. What are you going to do next?"

"I dunno." I shook my head.

Grammy made fun of me with that thick accent of hers, "'I dunno – I dunno.' What does that mean, even?"

"It means I acted before I thought it out all the way. Now I don't know how to fix it." Tears of frustration welled in my eyes.

"There is no fixing it. You cannot take it back. And so, you must figure out your next move. Like playing chess."

"I hate chess." I really did.

"You should play. It would teach you some patience. And strategy." She laughed as she said it because she knew it would never happen.

"Grammy, do you believe in powers?"

"What kind of powers? Like Superman? Like flying? Or like electricity?"

"I mean, like…" I had no idea where to start. "I mean, like, moving things with your mind. Or knowing what someone's thinking. Or…bringing back the dead."

"Ahhh, *yakiri*, I have seen so many things. I believe that anything can be possible. Sometimes, you have to believe with your heart, even if your eyes don't see. Then again, sometimes your eyes can see, and it is all a big lie." *Listen to that. She was a regular Yoda. You just had to flip her words around a little.*

"I'll figure this out. I just needed someone to know." I hugged her tight, breathing in the scent of Elizabeth Taylor's Passion and copious cups of strong, black tea.

"She is your cousin. She's family. Something good has to come out of it."

She sounded so damn sure.

# SHAR'N

*P* *eter called me Fleur.*
　　No one knew it was my real name except for me, him, and presumably Father. I said "presumably" because I'd never heard my father utter the word. Around a year ago I was digging through his books when I came across a handmade wooden box. It was hidden behind a bank of encyclopedias, tucked around the innermost corner of the shelf. Inside was a crocheted baby blanket in three shades of pink.

　　A name was painstakingly sewn into the middle using cross-stitch: "Fleur."

　　Also in the box was a sketch of who had to be my mother, because she looked too much like an image of grown-up-me to be otherwise. And there was a card. It was a sheet of thick paper folded in two, and the image of a beautiful flower was painted in watercolor on the front. I don't know what kind of flower it was because I've never seen one quite like it. All the colors of the rainbow were along its petals, like a colorful dew blessed them at daybreak.

Inside the clean folded paper was a lovely note:

*Oh, Dear Joseph,*

*She is almost here; I can feel it. We will be the luckiest parents, won't we? We will teach her all about the world, won't we? I can feel her moving, already curious. I've never doubted my decision to join The People, but now I am happier than ever that I made that choice. The choice to be with you, my love.*

*We shall call her Fleur. She will be the only one!*

*All of my love forever,*
*Lilly*

I was fairly certain my grandmother was the one who traded *Fleur* for *Rose of Sharon*. She had transformed me from extraordinary into less than nothing.

*Fleur* means "flower" in French. That name made me THE flower, not just one of countless Daisies, Roses, or Jasmines. I would have been the only flower that mattered. To my parents, at least.

It sounded lovely coming from Peter's lips. I don't remember ever hearing it out loud, except for the one whispered time I passed the story on to him: an illicit round of Telephone—a game we played in the lower grades, even though most of us had never seen one.

*Fleur.*

The laundry was dry, thanks to the constant warm breeze waving through the afternoon. Unclipping the underclothes, I placed them into the proper baskets. The yellowish envelope stood tightly tied underneath my worn checkered apron, begging for my attention.

Although the idea of having a family on The Outside thrilled me, I hadn't the faintest idea of how to begin correspondence. We didn't have a post office. Even if I wrote a response to her letter, there wasn't a way to deliver it. Besides, what would I say?

*Dear Cousin,*

*How are you? I am fine. Except I'm not allowed to touch anyone. Or read. Or really talk to anyone. I have one friend. He's a good one, but he's the only one.*

*I'm happy to answer any religious questions you might have.*

*Cheers,*
*Rose of Sharon*

*P.S. What do Otter Pops taste like? And Reese's?*

Hardly the start to a brand-new friendship.

# CHRYS

O kay. I felt a little bit better. Telling Grammy Esther about the letter made me feel like maybe I wasn't the most horrible, untrustworthy, wild teenager in the world. But I still needed to fix the situation. How was I going to do that?

I had nothing.

Mom was working late again. She tutored a man from Guatemala to help him improve his English, but he didn't get off work until almost seven so she usually wasn't home on Tuesdays and Thursdays until around nine. There was a huge stack of Lean Cuisines in the freezer for just that reason.

Unwrapping the square white box, I removed the plastic from a little round pizza and popped it in the microwave for three minutes. The instructions said to cook it for two minutes and forty-five seconds, but I'd found that the pepperoni gets just the right amount of crispy when you add that extra fifteen seconds.

Nothing on TV. News. More news. Stupid reruns of *Modern Family.* I guess I should have been reading *The Grapes of Wrath,* anyway. The pizza was hot, and it burned my fingers. I was starving but I was just going to have to wait until it cooled down a little bit.

*Grapes of Wrath,* Grapes of *Shmath.* Reading about these hungry people made me even more hungry.

"Hey Lauren." She picked up after the first ring, of course. She was always so desperate.

"Hey Chrys!" She seemed preoccupied.

"What's goin' on? What are you doing?" I pulled a stringy bit of cheese, but it kept pulling and pulling—pretty soon I had a cheesy ring around my middle finger. I popped it in my mouth.

"I'm trying to figure out what to wear. I'm so excited. Steven's gonna take me to *Five Guys* for burgers before the dance."

"Does Steven Ku drive?" That could come in handy.

"Yeaaaaah, why d'you need to know?" She sounded suspicious.

"I dunno, it's always good to know who has wheels." Indeed.

"What's up with you today, Chrys? You've been acting totally weird." She sighed like my weirdness was causing her a huge load of trouble.

"I'm not acting weird. You're acting weird. You're, like, obsessed with Steven Ku."

"Just because Brendan doesn't give you the time of day doesn't mean you have to act like a jerk." Ouch.

"Yeah, whatever, *Mrs. Lauren Ku*, I'll talk to you later." I hung up on her.

I hadn't even thought about Brendan at all during the day, 'cause I was so wrapped up in the whole letter thing.

It looked like I needed to get my priorities straight.

I texted Sadie with fingers that flew like an Olympic sprinter. Sadie had known Brendan since fourth grade.

**Me: Hi Sadie**

**Shady Sadie: Hi Chrys wassup?**

**Me: Do U have Brendans #????**

**Shady Sadie: Why, U takin the plunge?**

**Me: Yep**

**Shady Sadie: Good luck I heard he was gonna ask Amanda Lefler to the dance**

*Crap.*

**Me: O well its worth a try**

**Shady Sadie: OK call 4085559865 he has soccer tonite tho**

**Me: Thx**

**Shady Sadie: NP**

If I called while he was in soccer, I wouldn't have to have an awkward conversation with him. I could just leave a message and act cool about everything.

I dialed and got his voicemail. *Yahtzee!*

"Yo! This is B. Leave a message." My God, he sounded like a grown man.

43

"Uhm, hi." This was not going so well ALREADY. "This is, uhm, Chrysanthemum Perkins. Just wondering if you are already going to the dance with somebody." What next what next, what next? "So, yeaaaah. Callmebackokay, bye!"

What. A. Spazz.

And why did I use my whole name? Everyone knows me as "Chrys." He probably wouldn't even know who called him. He'd probably send me to voicemail any time I called now. I'd ruined everything, for EVER!

Even though I was named while we were living in that freak-o cult—sorry, Religious Community—Mom wanted me to keep it. She said that it sounded like us: Chrys-and-the-Mum.

When we first left, she was planning to change it, but found it so poetically ironic that The People had helped name me, and we were gone, but the name was reflective of our situation. Mostly I just went by "Chrys," but when I had to sign any legal documents or official papers, I used the whole thing.

Mom was in love with irony and being *reflective* about things because she was a writer.

# SHAR'N

T he sound woke me from a deep sleep. No one ever
entered my room. Ever. The smallest noise would
have awoken me, let alone the sound of someone barging
into the dark.

"Rose of Sharon, I need to speak with you." It was my
Father's voice. He so seldom spoke directly to me that it
paralyzed me for a second. I couldn't move, even though I
desperately would have liked to.

Hissing from a match sounded like an angry snake in
the quiet small space. Soon my lantern was glowing,
inviting familiar shadows to dance around us. I managed to
sit up, pulling the covers around me.

"Now then, show me the letter." Keeping a safe
distance, he unfurled his fingers and beckoned.

"Yes, Father." I felt for it under my pillow, and then
handed it over, not looking at him.

Reading the letter seemed to take decades. A small line
of sweat grew across my upper lip. Would he take my

treasure away? Would he beat me for something over which I had no control?

Finally, he finished. He didn't say a word, just tapped the letter across his hand, thinking.

"I don't believe," he paused, clearing his throat. "I don't believe it's an altogether bad idea for you to have contact with this girl."

Surprise twisted its silky tendrils inside my chest.

"It is obvious," he continued, "that she is not getting the information that she craves. If you limit your correspondence to teaching this girl the Word of God, then you may respond. You may not meet her in person. If you attempt to do so, you will be severely punished." Looking at my gloves, he winced.

"How?" I sounded a bit too eager and did my best to tone it down. "How Father, shall I respond to her? I don't know where to take my letter," I mumbled.

"John Junior will take it to The Outside for you. Get the letter to him, and it will find its way." Handing the letter back to me, he blew out the light and exited the room, gently closing the door behind him.

Had it really happened? Had my father come to my room to give me permission to write to my cousin? Miracle of miracles!

What would I write? What to say to a stranger who is also family? A stranger, who is family, who wants to know about God?

Which stories would keep her interested in the Bible? Was it even possible to keep her interested in The Good

Book? On The Outside, they watch movies and television. They are free to openly read whatever they choose. They surf the internet and play video games. How do I make God's Word interesting to someone who has so many options for entertainment? Would she think me simple-minded? Dull?

I decided to plan really carefully. Maybe Peter would have some insight because some of his brothers regularly went to The Outside. A few of them are over eighteen, so they help distribute the flowers. Surely he had heard many things about what people were like there.

Rolling and bunching up my pillow, I tried to get comfortable enough to fall back asleep. Too many questions twirled through my brain. *How was she my cousin? Why didn't she live in The People's Land? How old was she? How did she find me? How will—*

Finally, I drifted off.

# CHRYS

What if she doesn't write back? What if she thinks I'm some kind of weirdo, and she's afraid of me, so she just threw the letter away?

I should have been thinking about the dance on Friday, instead, because Brendan accepted my invitation (even though he admitted that, yeah, I sounded like a troll on my voicemail). A couple of girls were totally pissed off at me now, but I thought it would be worth it. Luckily, Brendan was friends with Steven Ku so we were going to be double dating with Lauren, who was convinced that we should dress in coordinating colors. I wasn't sold on it yet. She wanted to go to the mall, but I had a ton of homework due by Friday.

I found out that I was getting a B- in math, which would make my mother freak out. If I could finish an extra credit packet that I picked up I thought I could swing at least a B+. But I guess that meant I would have to actually take the packet out of my backpack and look for a pencil.

Getting into homework mode, I pulled my dark hair up in a fat, messy bun on the top of my head. I dug my favorite comfy sweatpants out of a pile in the middle of my room and borrowed a big T-shirt from my mom's closet.

Okay, okay, I didn't normally have a homework uniform. I was just stalling.

*If she writes back, how do I continue to communicate with her? How can I ask her what I want to know without alarming her, or the other people who might read my words?*

I guessed the Bible stuff was a good start. No one would freak out about the Bible, right? From what I knew, those people lived like the Bible is an operating manual for life. They only wore clothes that were handmade, down to the woven fabric. They didn't use any kind of technology. They were only allowed to eat things that had been sent by God. Sounded pretty sad—no Cheetos, no McNuggets, no Slurpees.

The guys that came into town must have had phones or something. Otherwise, how did they take their orders? And let me tell you, those flowers were freakin' *everywhere*. You couldn't even go to the dentist without seeing a vase full of them. I didn't know what kind of flower it was, but it was big and fluffy, sort of like a monster dandelion on steroids. They came in just about any color you could imagine.

Every week the men in their funny straw hats drove horse-driven carriages full of flowers into town. There were five or six carriages, with three or four people on board.

They parked at the end of a street and unloaded into smaller pushcarts, which were rolled around until they were empty. The flowers were wrapped in muslin bags, which were taken back with the men once they'd dropped off the bouquets.

Mom always got a funny look on her face when she caught a glimpse of the carriages. She didn't quite hide, but she would step out of full view—like she was afraid one of the men might recognize her and drag her back to The People's Land.

I didn't think there was a thing in the world that she feared more.

# SHAR'N

W*hich name shall I use?*
I mulled it over for a while, deciding to stick with Rose of Sharon. How I ached to sign the letter with my real name. However, my writing would undoubtedly be monitored, and I could not even begin to imagine what would happen if my father found out I had been looking through his private belongings.

Because it was a school week, I could wake before dawn and have a little bit of free time. On Harvest weeks we began our work in the dark, and we returned in time for dinner preparations.

I lit my lantern and pulled out a fresh sheet of paper from my school satchel. We were encouraged to use as little paper as possible, because it was made by the teachers. Very different from the paper that my cousin's (my cousin! How strange it feels to think of her that way!) ink adorned. Her paper was white and impossibly smooth. Mine was tan and bumpy, the pulp not pressed quite flat. I had a pot of ink and a pen on my scarred, broken desk. One of the legs had found an unlikely departure before my time. A thick branch was wedged into its place, held fast with twine. Careful not to spill or drip the ink, I began to write.

*Dear Chrys,*

*I am ever so glad that you contacted me. I did not know that I had a cousin. I would be very pleased to be your religion tutor.*

*First lesson: In your letter, you wrote, "I have a desire to know God. I just don't know where to find him." Whenever you use the pronoun "he" or "him" or "his" when writing about God, it must always be capitalized.*

*I will be glad to help you find Him. Do you own a Bible? If you do not, I may be able to secure one for you.*

*Have a blessed day,*
*Rose of Sharon*

If I skipped breakfast, I could deliver the letter to John Junior on my way to school. There were so many butterflies in my stomach that I didn't feel even the slightest bit hungry. Stealing into the kitchen before anyone was offended by my presence, I wrapped a hunk of bread and an apple for lunch, depositing them into my school bag.

Many of the houses along the way were still dark, everyone asleep inside. The moon peeked eerily through a smear of grey clouds. I felt strange, as if the moon knew my new secret and was monitoring my careful steps.

A single lantern burned in the kitchen at John Senior's house. Wives bustled inside, beginning to cook breakfast and pack lunches.

John Senior had seven wives, ranging in age from seventeen to fifty. There were over twenty children between them all. Most of the oldest children were already married. One of the daughters, Alyssum, was married just over a month ago to a man in his late thirties, Tall Mark. John Senior's home was one of the largest in our community, a sprawling house with a wraparound porch. Now Alyssum lived in a small house with two other women and their offspring.

John Junior was the oldest Hawkins child, and the only son. He wasn't married, which is very unusual for any man over twenty, in The People's Land. There were whispers about not being able to produce children or having some kind of disability that couldn't be seen. The truth was that he led the delivery business, and just didn't have time for any distractions. He accepted calls to his cellular phone (the only modern technology allowed in our community), and created a detailed, complicated order and delivery schedule. Part of his job was to monitor how many flowers were planted and picked.

He was a handsome man, somewhere in his thirties. The lines around his eyes looked like they grew from smiling, not anger. His father, John Senior, looked like a strange, aged version of his son. There were hundreds of lines on his face, but I doubted that even one came from merriment.

Oh, the stories that were told about the things that took place at the Hawkins house! Tales of wives being beaten for not folding clothing correctly. Girls being starved because they burned dinner. The Hawkins girls in my grade level had serious, drawn faces. They sat quietly and jumped whenever a loud noise erupted, such as when a book or a door slammed closed. Even the younger ones sat with hunched shoulders, never running about the field with the other girls their age. Scandalous whispers sometimes wondered about two wives who disappeared years ago. There one day, gone the next. No one knew what happened to them, but it was speculated that John Sr. may have used too heavy of a hand in physically instructing them how to behave. Or too heavy a switch, a hose, or a belt. There had been no investigations, and even the families of the women stopped talking about it after a time. The gossip I heard whispered between my father's wives made me very nervous to knock on the door.

I worked up the courage to rap lightly on the door and could hear shuffling inside. It opened just an inch. A girl around twenty presented an eye, looking up and down at the person visiting before daybreak. Her swollen, pregnant body strained against the jam. It seemed like all women who were a part of The People were constantly in one state of pregnancy or another. My family was no different.

"Yes?" It wasn't polite, nor impolite. It was a question, but it sounded defeated. Dead.

"I...I need to give something to...to John Junior. To bring into town." My teeth chattered with cold and nerves. The eye widened in alarm, so I added, "My father sent me."

She closed the door, and I heard a male voice join the many pitches within.

Then it opened wide and standing in its frame was John Senior.

His hair was white and fell along his shoulders, a brittle waterfall. In my mind I compared him to a photograph that I saw on the back of Father's copy of *Tom Sawyer*. John Senior bore more than a passing resemblance to Mark Twain. His nose was sharp and dangling beneath it was a great walrus's mustache. He was thin, much thinner than I expected him to be. Rough-hewn pants sagged on his hips, cinched with a leather belt.

John Senior twirled his mustache with a bony finger, studying me.

"Well, say! Yer that bush child, aren't ye? Dark Joseph's girl!"

I nodded my head and willed my eyes to stop staring at his yellow, pitted teeth, framed by a strangely menacing smile.

"Look at ye, darlin'. All grown up! How old are ye now?" He kept twirling, twirling, twirling that unfortunate facial hair.

"I'll be sixteen next month," I mumbled.

"Sixteen! Well, I'll be! Seems like just yesterday ye were toddlin' through The Harvest! Ha! Sixteen! Anybody spoken for ye, yet?"

The women working in the kitchen behind him froze.

"N-no s-sir," I stuttered.

Reaching for a handkerchief, he coughed violently.

"Well," he winked, "a pretty girl like ye'll find somebody without any problem at all."

His wives looked up in shock. I saw two of them draw the sign of the cross in the air. One shielded her ready-for-delivery stomach, as if I might have attacked her. A few glared in my direction.

"I-I came to see John Junior." My heart raced. "Please," I added hastily.

"What do you want with that young buck? Ye got plans with my boy?" I hated the way he made it sound so dirty.

"No!" *Calm down, Fleur! A little quieter, now.* "My father sent me. I need to have a letter delivered to The Outside."

"Funny," the old man said, "ye and my boy have something big in common..."

Thankfully, John Junior appeared in the door frame next to his father, wiping his hands on a towel. He was still chewing some of his breakfast.

"I was just about to tell Shar'n, here, about how ye two got somethin' in common. Ye see, Shar'n, John Junior done killed his mama, just like ye. Couple a murderers here on my porch. Nothin' like breakin' a commandment or two!" Bursting into cold hearted laughter, John Senior slapped his knee.

The smell of eggs and sausage emanating from the

Hawkins kitchen made my stomach growl loud enough for the men to hear.

John Senior laughed again, and then barked, "Hibiscus! Get this girl somethin' to eat. Move it, woman."

John Junior looked at me questioningly.

"Sir, I need to have a letter delivered to The Outside. My father told me to give it to you." I pulled the folded page out of my bag and extended it to him.

John Senior snatched it up quicker than I would have believed his old arms could move. Opening it, he began to read out loud, but then finished in silence.

"Very interesting, bush girl. Ye givin' Bible lessons to this child?"

"Well, yes. Father said it was all right. I have his permission. He thinks that it is good to spread God's Word to those who don't have any other way to find it." The syllables tripped over my tongue, sounding slow and garbled.

"Mmmhmmm. Well, Junior, what're ye waitin' for? Some Outsider is waitin' for a delivery!" John Senior laughed heartily, revealing many gaps where molars had once been. He leaned his head outside and spat, bringing on another fit of meaty coughing.

"Shar'n, I'll deliver this when I bring out the carriages this morning. Do you have an address? I don't know where to take it." His voice was smooth and very kind.

"Well, I– yes." I turned the envelope over. I reused the one that came with the delivery, just crossed out the mailing information. It was still visible, though, and he stared at it for a few seconds.

"Perfect, thanks."

"You don't need to write it down?" I asked, uncertain. I wanted my letter to reach its intended recipient.

"I've got it up here." He tapped his forehead. I absolutely believed him.

"Well, okay. Thank you." As I was backing away, John Senior's quick arm made another appearance, snatching my elbow and dragging me back to the door.

"Silly, silly girl! He doesn't need to write it down! He's got it right there on the envelope."

I felt so stupid. I should have thought of that already, and the way John Senior laughed made it so much worse.

"Just you wait," he ordered. "Hibiscus! Where's that food?"

A small, beaten-down looking woman with thinning, stringy hair appeared. Her face was already lined, though I'd have guessed her to be in her twenties. She handed me a cloth bundle, raw hate in her eyes.

Looking at the wooden boards beneath my feet, I thanked her. Holding it far from her body, she thrust the food away from her chest.

"Those gloves," her husband drawled, "nice quality. Very finely made."

"Thank you." I felt his gaze burning through the soft leather.

"Best be off to school now, Shar'n." He smiled once again, giving me a glimpse of rot.

I turned and ran.

For some reason I cried. I wasn't even sure why. Sobs built in the pit of my stomach, ripping through my chest, surfacing on my dry lips. I looked inside the wrapped cloth, finding two slices of bacon and a thick slice of buttered toast.

Walking the rest of the way to school, I ate my ill-gotten breakfast.

I couldn't taste a bite of it.

# CHRYS

I hated shopping with Lauren. We had similar tastes, but she was so freakin' indecisive that I usually wanted to stab myself in the eye with a fork by the time we finally left the mall. She decided that our color for the dance would be teal. I let her pick because she was being pretty cool about letting us all ride in Steven's car, when I could tell she would rather be alone with him all night.

I found a teal tank top and a teal denim skirt right away. Lauren had gone back and forth from Forever Twenty-One and Gap around a billion times, trying to decide between a tank dress and a T-shirt and shorts. It was killing me. I left her and went to Starbucks for an iced tea, and she didn't even notice.

"I just don't know." She bit her thumbnail, looking up and down at the dress.

"Just pick something, please."

"Hey, where'd you get the Starbucks?"

"At Starbucks."

"You know what I mean, Chrys!"

"See, you didn't even notice I was gone." I rolled my eyes at her.

"I guess the dress is cuter. Can I wear it to school after, though? Or is it too fancy?"

Here we go, again.

"Lauren," I sighed, "it's cute. You can totally wear it to school after."

She nodded and headed into the store to finally make her purchase.

When her mom dropped me off at home, Grammy Esther poked her head out of her door after she heard me in the hallway.

"Come in," she ordered. She was up to something.

Lying on her coffee table was the envelope I mailed less than a week ago.

Disappointment washed over me, surprising me with its intensity. The mailing address must not have worked. Apparently, you had to have more information than a parent's name and nutty commune title to get something mailed in our country, *go figure.*

"Oh, well." I tried my hardest to act like I didn't care, but it sounded really fake.

"What do you mean? Look closer!" Grammy shuffled to the table, her fuzzy lime-green slippers looked like frantic creatures stumbling across the hardwood floor.

Picking up the envelope, she handed it to me as I approached. The address had been crossed out in black ink. So had all the other information. Written in scrolling letters on one of the blank spots was my name.

"I was here when the man delivered it. He was going to put it into your mail slot, but I convinced him to hand it over to me. I wasn't sure if your mother should see it." *I love you, Grammy!*

I thanked her and opened it. It had been resealed somehow, and inside was a sheet of rough paper. You could see bits of pulp bumping the dark, creased page. It reminded me of the fancy stationery that I saw in a shop downtown, only that paper had little flowers mixed in.

Grammy Esther managed to wait somewhat patiently for me to finish reading. She sat on the couch with her legs crossed, the dancing green furry beasts on her feet the only clue of her eagerness to hear about what I'd received.

"Well," I told her, "I'm supposed to capitalize 'Him' when I'm talking about God."

"You should have already known that."

"And she wants to know if I need a Bible."

"Tell her yes. I want to see what their Bibles look like. I have heard that they are different than the average Good Book. You know that women aren't supposed to read anything but the Bible in that place?" She sounded disgusted. Like my mother, Grammy loved to read. She was always pushing the classics on me, like *Jane Eyre* and *Wuthering Heights*. I could never get past the first few pages. It's like they were written in a different language or something.

"No kidding."

"That's what I've heard. The men can read, but not the

women." She shook her head at the absurdity of it.

"Maybe I should move there. Then I wouldn't have to read *The Grapes of Wrath*." I said it just to annoy her.

"Don't say such things! You are so lucky to be able to read books like that. When I was young, in the camps, we were not allowed books. Life is a hard thing to bear without the escape of words. Literature can take you away from any sort of prison, even if just for a few hours."

When she put it that way, it made me feel so guilty.

"I'll ask for the book. And I'll make sure to capitalize 'Him.' What did the man look like?"

"Handsome but for the strange clothes. He had a kind face." I wanted more details from her, but I could tell that was all I was gonna get.

Thanking her, I kissed her cheek. She let me know that I would be coming back to her apartment with Mom for dinner. Roast beef. My favorite Grammy Esther dinner.

Tucking the envelope into my shopping bag, I crossed the hall, finding my mother at the computer, as usual.

"Hi, Honey!" She called out without turning around, her fingers dancing across the keyboard at impossible speed. "Anything cool happen today?"

"Not really," I answered.

I really hated lying to her, but I couldn't seem to stop.

# SHAR'N

It was impossible to concentrate in class. I wondered if
the letter had already reached its destination. Maybe my
cousin had already answered. Would the response come to
the school again? *Will I be able to survive waiting through
the day of boring, repetitive lectures until I could open it?*

My hands sweated inside their casings. Mr. Adams
droned on and on about how we, as women, were expected
to live out our lives. I already knew God's plan for me from
years of hearing this very lecture. Babies. Lots and lots of
them. Although there was some doubt in my mind about
finding someone to father them, as I was pretty sure there
wouldn't be any volunteers. That sort of thing requires
actually touching someone. I know all about it because
some of Father's reading selections can get pretty racy. I
guess I should be thankful that I scare everyone away. I
wondered how much my classmates knew about the
process. Very little, I was sure—not that they would ever
confide in me, and I had no idea what, if anything, mothers

told their daughters to prepare them for it.

How could the other girls listen to this time and again and still appear to be interested, nodding their heads with small, pleasant smiles on their lips? Maybe because they didn't know about the women I'd read about; women who worked, travelled, and did amazing things—without marrying or having babies. I squirmed in my seat, trying to picture Amelia Earhart with twelve kids, bent over picking flowers.

One of the series on the bookshelf starred a woman detective who ran around with a gun, solving murders and having love affairs. If the other pupils sitting around me knew about her, would they be so terribly excited about what was in store for them? No wonder we weren't supposed to read that sort of thing. Flowers were nowhere near as exciting as spying on people and chasing them around in the dark. *And the idea that we could be the ones doing the spying and chasing?* Who would pick all the flowers every other week?

When lunch time finally rolled around, I didn't feel much like talking.

"Come on, Shar'n. What's eating you?" Peter asked me.

"It's the God's plan lecture, again."

"And?"

"And it's not His plan for me. It can't be." For some reason I felt like crying.

"Don't worry, someone is out there for you. There is someone for everyone." He sounded so sure. He didn't understand what I was saying. At all.

I didn't answer him, just picked at my muffin, sprinkling my skirt with crumbs. Peter looked worried.

"Meet me at the barn?"

"After I take out the garbage." I stood up and dusted off the bread particles, leaving a snack for the birds.

"Sure. I'll wait for you there."

I didn't say goodbye.

After school, I gathered the garbage that belonged in the fire pit: bits of paper, scraps of dried things. The bucket of food trash was heavy, and it sloshed as it bumped against my legs. The pig trough was a short walk down the road from our house, but when you were carrying a few days' worth of smelly leftovers, it seemed like miles.

Rounding the corner of the barn where all the cows were kept, I heard laughter drifting across the grass. Low murmuring followed. Someone was behind the barn.

The pigs were happy to see me. I filled their trough, then exited their pen as they began to eat with loud sloppy bites. Above the slurping, I heard more laughter.

Holding the empty bucket, I quietly crept along the side of the barn. I should have just walked away, but one of the voices was familiar, and I just couldn't make my feet begin the short trek back to the house. Keeping my back against the splintery wall, I took small sideways steps until I reached the end of the line. Leaning out, I quickly peeked around the side.

It was a girl from my grade. Her name was Jasmine, and she had loads of friends. And a mean streak. If you asked an adult to give you their opinion on the girl, they would no doubt gush about how wonderful she was. She always sat still during lectures. She always looked as pretty as a picture. She always said the right things. The truth was, she knew how perfect the facade was and she used it to her advantage. I'd seen her tease younger children, and bully other girls into giving her things from their lunches. One day I heard her compliment another girl in our class about a ribbon in her hair. The next day, Jasmine was wearing the ribbon. There was no doubt that it wasn't a gladly given gift.

The boy she was with was a Luke. Young Luke. It was a funny name because he may have been Young Luke when he was little, but there were another two Lukes now, and he was older than they were. Jasmine and Luke lay on their backs, on the grass. She had her head resting on his shoulder, and he played with her curly hair, wrapping it around his finger and pulling it lazily across his cheek.

Even though I was certain she would do something awful if she saw me, I couldn't look away. He murmured in her ear, then leaned over, shifting her head to the ground. They shared a deep kiss, one that made it fairly obvious that they had practiced often. What would happen to them if they were reported? Her father would probably beat her.

I felt a strange surge of power at the prospect of knowing her secret.

She moaned and reached up, burying her fingers into his blonde hair, pulling him closer.

I carefully slid back along the wall and made my way

home, eager to share this news with Peter.

He wasn't impressed.

"How did you know?" I asked him, exasperated.

"Because," he told me, "Luke has a gigantic mouth. Not just for kissing Jasmine, either. He is more than happy to tell us boys all about it."

"But that could get them in a lot of trouble! Why would he risk it?" It made no sense to me.

"He wants us all to know how special he is. Not a lot of girls would do that, you know. And Jasmine is a girl that a lot of boys would like to kiss."

"What about you?" I searched his face.

"Huh?"

"Do you want to kiss her?" *Why did my chest ache when I asked?*

"Definitely not," he laughed.

Relief spilled through my veins like cold water.

"Now, about God's plan for you..." Peter smirked.

"Never mind. Only He knows his plan for me. And I'm pretty sure that it's not the same as Jasmine's plan. Or anyone else's for that matter."

Peter quirked an eyebrow at me, but he didn't push. When the tree-canopied light around us turned nature's late-afternoon orange, he helped me up from our seat in the deserted barn's shade.

"Hey, look." He pointed to an unmoving bird, lying on its side in the grass.

I didn't know much about birds, but I believe it was some sort of jay.

"Will you?" Peter put his hands on his knees, bending over to get a closer look.

"I'll try." I shuffled off my gloves, laying my hands on the creature. It was very cold.

The tips of my fingers buzzed like they had fallen asleep, but the sensation didn't go any further. I heard the faintest whisper of what had happened to the bird. Scattered words filled my head.

"He's been gone too long." It made me sad that I couldn't bring him back. "He was just old. I don't think could he fly any longer."

"We should bury him." Peter took off his hat, rolled up his sleeves, and used his big hands to dig in the earth.

We had a nice hole within minutes. I held the bird for a moment, stroking its dull blue feathers. Even the tiny prickles that had once been at my fingertips were now gone. I placed him in his grave, and Peter covered him, patting the dirt into firmness as he did it.

"Will you say a prayer?" I dusted my hands against my skirt. I put my gloves back on then folded my hands in front of me.

"Dear Lord," Peter began, "welcome this creature into Your arms. He has come to be with You at Your house, as we all will someday. Amen."

"Thank you, that was nice." I squeezed his arm.

"We better get home." He looked up at the darkening sky.

I arrived at the house as my family was finishing dinner. Meal sounds filled the small kitchen, two long tables taking up most of the space. I heard children's voices, clinking silverware, chairs scraping as bodies rose to fill their plates or excuse themselves from the table. My father's low voice rumbled but couldn't discern what he was saying.

A bowl of stew sat on the edge of the porch with a square of cornbread beside it. When my family thanked the Lord for their meals, they held hands around the tables. I just said a quick word of thanks in my head. Leaning against a beam, I sat alone, as usual, and ate my meal. When I was finished, I left the empty bowl and headed around to the back of the house.

Only the door to my bedroom awaited my return.

# CHRYS

I wrote her back! I told her that, yeah, I wanted a Bible—just so Grammy Esther could check it out—and I wanted to know about her. What did she like to do? What were her favorite things? I kept it short, 'cause I tend to ramble and I didn't want to freak her out. I told her that I love music. I didn't tell her that I hated reading, because that seemed mean if she wasn't allowed to do it. Okay, I didn't really hate reading. I just preferred reading stuff that I *like*. Which was *not The Grapes of Wrath*. I read all the *Hunger Games*, even before the movies started coming out. I also read the first *Divergent*. See? I wasn't totally ignorant. I just didn't want to read all the stuff that my mom and Grammy were always telling me to read.

Last weekend was the dance, but I didn't think I should write about that because I was pretty sure they didn't have dances at The People's Land. Unless it was for like, teenagers dancing with old men or something.

So, Steven and Lauren were an actual thing, all of a

sudden. They spent the night connected at the hip, looking all starry-eyed while they danced the night away. She said they kissed after they dropped us off, but that was all.

Well, I kissed Brendan, too, which took some of the wind out of her sails. She was excited that it happened to her, telling me about how magical it was and everything. I guess I should have let her keep it, but it wasn't like it was a huge deal.

When she and Steven dropped Brendan and me off at my house, I brought him to Mom's room to introduce them. Her door was wide open wide. She was wearing her bedtime sweatpants, hair pulled into a messy ponytail, looking like she could have been at the dance, she seemed so young. Propped up against the headboard, she was reading something with a pen hanging out of her mouth. It seemed like she was always writing notes in the books that she liked to read—which was one reason that we didn't use the library all that often.

"Hey, Mom, this is Brendan."

Looking up from the book, a wide smile crept across her face, "Well, hello, Brendan, very nice to meet you!" The grin made her look even more like a teenager.

"Uh, hi," Brendan said, sounding uncomfortable.

"Okay, sooo, we're gonna go to the living room and make out for a while, so I'll see ya later."

"Sure, Honey." She had already returned to reading.

I closed her door.

"No second base!" She yelled from behind it.

Brendan was clearly shocked that I shared these words

with my mother. I should admit that I had the conversation to freak him out because I thought it would be funny.

And it totally was.

"You always talk to your mom like that?" he asked.

"Yeah, totally. She's cool."

"I'll say..." He looked in the direction of Mom's room, but I pulled him down to the couch, turning on the TV.

"I thought we were gonna make out?"

I did end up kissing him. It was alright. Turned out he's kind of a noisy kisser, though.

Brendan left to walk home, since he lived close by. After I saw him out, I stopped at Mom's room again. She was already asleep, tucked in tight.

"Oh Mom," I whispered, "how mad would you be if I told you about the letters?"

Again, I felt totally guilty. I had the hardest time getting to sleep, and when I did, I dreamed that we lived back at The People's Land. We were kept chained up so we wouldn't run away again. My cousin brought us our dinner, and said, "You never should have run away." It was so freaky, but it felt real and I couldn't wake up.

The next day was Saturday and Mom didn't have to work. She told me to pack up for the beach. I grabbed a swimsuit and a towel, tied my hair up in a bun, and tried to find my flip flops.

The doorbell rang.

When my mom answered the door, she sounded totally surprised, so I rushed to see who our visitor was. When I saw who was standing at our door I almost had a heart attack.

*CRAP! Crapcrapcrapcrapcrapcrapcrap.*

The man held his straw hat in his hands, fists clenched around the brim. His black leather shoes shifted along our welcome mat. My mother was holding a package wrapped in white fabric with string tied around it, like a birthday present.

"Yes, well…" Mom aimed her eyes at the floor.

"Well." The man tried to search her downward-pointing face.

"Goodbye, then." Mom reached for the doorknob, a visual cue that she was ready for him to go.

"Goodbye, Iris."

"I'm not Iris, anymore, John. I'm Catherine, now. Again."

"Goodbye, Catherine."

They seemed frozen in place for an awkward minute, and then he turned and left. She closed the door behind him.

"I know you're there, Chrys."

She turned to me, eyes blazing with fury.

"*What have you done?!*"

"I–I wanted to meet my cousin, Mom. We don't have any family, but she's there, and I–"

"I am your family. Grammy is your family. This is ridiculous! You're putting us at risk! I have no idea what they'll do now that they know where we live!"

"But Mom–"

"No. I don't want to hear about any of this. Keep it away from me."

"You don't understand, Mom –"

"Here's what I understand, Chrysanthemum: I got us away from that place. I struggled. I fought to keep us safe, to create a life for us. And you've just gone and thrown it away!" Tears were in her eyes now, making me feel awful.

She pushed the package into my arms, ran to her bedroom, and slammed the door.

*Guess we're not going to the beach after all.*

I didn't know what to do. What if I had just given away our secret hiding spot? What if they did come to get us?

*Crap.*

Only Grammy Esther would be able to help me figure this one out.

I knocked on her door, and it opened immediately, as if she had been waiting for me.

Which she had.

"Thin walls," she explained.

"My Mom. She's so mad at me, Grammy!"

"Yes, yes, I know. Now open the package."

The string looked like it was tied in a knot, but when I pulled a loose end, it untied. Inside the fabric wrapper was a thick Bible, with what looked like a stiff, black leather cover. The title, *The People's Bible,* was embossed in gold ink.

I opened the cover, and another one of those bumpy sheets of paper fell out. I read aloud:

*Dear Chrys,*

*This Bible will help us with our lessons. I marked the chapter that I would like you to read first. If you have any questions, please include them in your next letter.*

*I liked hearing about you. I would like to hear more. How can we live without our lives? How will we know it's us without our past?*

*As for me, there isn't a lot to tell. I keep busy with school and The Harvest, most of the time. This must sound strange to you. One half of the world cannot understand the pleasures of the other.*

*If you work hard at your studies, God will protect you. Get smart and nothing can touch you.*

*I'm so glad that you contacted me, Chrys. If there's just one kind of folks, why can't they get along with each other? If they're all alike, why do they go out of their way to despise each other?*

*Enjoy your reading,*
*Rose of Sharon*

"Okay," I started, "that was the weirdest letter I've ever gotten."

"People do speak differently in that place, don't they?" Grammy spoke slowly, thoughtfully.

"What is it, Grammy?" *Something was definitely up.*

Well," she began, "I am seeing quotes."

*Huh?*

"At the bottom, there, 'If there's just one kind of folks...' that's from *To Kill a Mockingbird*. Harper Lee. I know it." She scanned the sheet. "And up a little bit, 'Get smart and no one can touch you.' That's from something, too, I just can't remember what." She was getting excited, now. "'One half of the world cannot understand the pleasures of the other,' That's from Jane Austen's *Emma*! And," she read slowly, 'How can we live without our lives? How will we know it's us without our past?' You will never believe what book that quote is from." She looked at me expectantly.

"Okay, fine, I'll bite. Where is the quote from, Grammy?" I rolled my eyes.

"Your very own *The Grapes of Wrath*."

"What does it all mean?" I wondered out loud.

"It means," Grammy Esther answered, "this girl likes to read."

# FLEUR

# 1

My back felt like it was broken, and my feet were filled with a fierce ache. Harvest week. The day was long and hot, and the Field Master had it in for me, for some reason.

"Shar'n! Pick faster!"

"Shar'n! Slowin' down, are we?"

"Shar'n! Not many flowers in that bucket!"

Jasmine was picking in the row directly in front of me, and every time I got yelled at, she would turn her head and smirk. I wondered how long that smirk would last if I told her what I had seen her doing with Luke behind the barn.

Harvest weeks are never fun, and it always felt like you'd finally recovered by the end of a school week—just in time to pick again. Females under ten and over fifty were excused, so on the bright side, I only had about thirty-five more years of it to endure. One mother from each household got to stay home with the kids. They took turns. It might have been one of the only reasons that I'd like to be a mother.

The Field Master discouraged gossip, and it would have been difficult to talk to the others anyway, because everyone was facing someone else's back most of the time. The hours were usually passed by singing. The only music allowed in The People's Land was religious music, hymns that we learn in church on Sundays. By the end of the week, everyone had either a burned or tanned face and a voice hoarse from all the singing. Except for me. I never sang.

We only planted one kind of flower, the Opus Dei. The stems are long and thick, and we were trained to cut them at exactly one and a half inches up from the soil. The head of the flower was large and round, like a pompom, and they grew in every color that you could imagine. It was all very beautiful to see—just before we began to snip them away. Like a sea of rainbows, the fields were so bright with them that they were almost blinding under the sun.

There were four fields that were planted and harvested in rotation, year-round. The flowers took less than one month to grow into mature blooms. I walked down the path between the fields on my way to school, and a field on its way to being ready was a truly wonderful thing to see.

Because boys were required to attend school full-time until they were eighteen years old, most of the men seeded the land between trips to The Outside to make their deliveries. The men who didn't plant or make deliveries were the ones who worked in the painted building.

Our homes were natural wood colored. The barns were

too, for the most part. There were one or two white ones from long ago, but no one had painted a barn or a home in many, many years. The school had the vestiges of an ancient paint job, strips of flaky green that cracked and fell from the building from time to time. Eventually it would return to its natural state, I imagined. The only building that was painted was the business office, which was a muted blue. My father worked in that building, along with a few others who studied the flowers, and John Junior, who was in charge of taking orders and scheduling deliveries.

Women were not allowed in that building under any circumstances. When wives brought hot lunches to the men who worked inside, they stood at the door until the food had been collected.

The sun was almost down, making the world look like it did when I began to work in the morning. Sitting on the porch, eating my dinner of chicken and mixed vegetables, I wondered how Peter was doing. One of the hardest things about Harvesting was not seeing my friend all week. I imagined him sitting alone at lunch. I wished I could have sat behind the abandoned barn with him during the afternoon, instead of picking. Picking. Picking. Picking. And seeing Jasmine's mean smile.

The wives had been taking their turns in the tub since we returned. I usually waited until everyone was in bed to do my bathing, so I didn't accidentally offend someone by happening to be in their path. I was too tired to wait and decided to use the water pump in the yard to wash my hands and face. We'd all be out there sweating again in a few hours, anyway. What was the point of becoming clean?

The water felt so wonderful splashing through my bare hands, running down my neck. My apron was filthy, but it was the only thing I had to dry with, so it would have to do.

"Psssst," a little voice called to me from the bushes. "Shar'n! Over here, Shar'n!"

I could see Wee Lilac's shining face, illuminated by the almost-full moon.

"What are you up to, Lilac?" She was the only person in my family who spoke to me, other than Father. She was only five; smart enough to know she's supposed to shun me, but young enough to want to give me a chance. While we were at school, she was a stranger. When she walked in the group with our siblings, I was ignored. Whenever she could steal a second alone with me, she was quick to grasp it.

"Nothin'." She grinned, looking like she was missing more teeth than she had standing. "I got Cat." She lifted Cat out of the bushes. My pet was draped over her arm, looking bored.

The animal deserved a better, more creative name. However, when trying to select one, the only choices that popped into my head were of the literary nature. Captain Ahab was the first. Nicholas Nickleby was the second. Since I wasn't supposed to have been exposed to those characters, Cat seemed like a safe alternative.

"How was school?" I asked her. The younger ones got to go full-time while we picked.

"Alright." Wee Lilac was not a huge fan of organized

education.

"You should go back in before they catch you."

"They never catch me, Shar'n. I'm too quick," she giggled.

"Well, I'm off to bed. It was a very, very long day." As if on cue, I yawned. Cat meowed in sympathy.

"I know. It's what they're all sayin' inside, too. I'm the one with all the energy!" And she disappeared.

It was a short conversation, but it was always nice when someone was willing to talk to me. It made me feel like a human being, instead of a contagious disease to be avoided.

## 2

After another long day of Harvesting, I returned home to find the Bible on my bed. It was wrapped up the way it was when I sent it to The Outside, the string tied in a knotted bow at the top. I had taken the Bible from the church, where a tall stack of them always stood on the inside of the front double doors waiting for a new home.

I wondered who had the courage to enter my room. It had to have been Father. I couldn't imagine one of the wives being adventurous enough to even touch my door, and the children had all been expressly forbidden to approach the back of the house.

Relishing the action of untying the package even though I already knew what was inside, I wondered why she had returned it to me. I thought I was being a little bit clever in my note, telling her that I had marked a chapter for her to read. I marked the first page with a bit of string, telling her to start with book of Genesis, at the very beginning. My plan was for her to read the books in order, asking questions about what she had read, and then I could answer them.

The glow from the lantern made shadows bounce along the cover. I found her response on another sheet of the beautiful bright paper, and ran my hands along the front of it, marveling at its smoothness.

A rap at my door caused me to jump, dropping the note to the ground.

"Ah, come in." I scrambled to pick up the sheet.

My Father, looking uncomfortable as usual, stepped halfway through the door. It was as if he were afraid the room would swallow him up if he entered all the way.

"John Junior brought the package back for you. The girl found him on the street and gave it to him."

"Oh. I was wondering how it came to be here."

"Why did she return the book to you?" He just couldn't quite look into my eyes, lingering around my nose or upper lip.

"Well," I explained, "I'm not entirely sure, just yet. I was about to read her letter when you arrived."

He nodded his head, encouraging me to share the information written within.

"She says that she's a note-taker. She writes inside the books that she studies," I began. "She has lots of questions about the book of Genesis but had to send the book back so that I could read them and answer them."

This seemed to make sense to my father.

"What else does she say?" He was strangely curious, showing more interest than he'd shown in me during my lifetime.

"She understands that I would like her to read in order, but she skipped around a little bit, and would like me to look at her notes in the back of the book, too." I looked up to find him staring at my uncovered hands, holding the message. Almost imperceptibly, he took a step backward, further out of the room.

"This sounds fine. Bring your response to John Junior when you are ready." Then he was gone.

I hadn't revealed everything that was included in the note. For example, I didn't tell him that she had written, "I enjoyed reading your letter. I am interested, also, in being able to quote the Bible." The word "quote" was pressed so hard into the page that it was embossed on the other side. It was also underlined. Twice. So, my cousin had understood my coded message!

Also forcefully written were the words "I am very interested in the last part of this book." I opened the book, flipping to the back cover. I'm not sure what I expected to find, but it most was most certainly not what I discovered.

My cousin had defiled the Bible. She had carved out a rectangular hunk of pages. Inside the shallow hole was something wrapped in thin, crinkly white paper.

I slowly unwrapped the mysterious contraband, finding a hard, black, flat...thing. On the front of it was a small, square sheet of yellow paper that was somehow sticking onto the item. I pulled the paper off, finding a strip of adhesive at the top. Very clever! I read what was written:

"Turn it on"

Looking closer, I found buttons. None of them were marked as "On." I pressed them all until a light filled the front of the item. It startled me and I dropped it onto the bed.

*What kind of insanity is this?* I'd only read about technology. I knew this wasn't a television. I supposed it could be a telephone, but I didn't see any numbers on it.

A list of novels appeared. Some that I've already read. A couple, like *To Kill a Mockingbird,* I'd read more than once. I loved the way that Scout learned about life. And I loved how warm and gentle the father, Atticus, was. I also sort of related to Boo Radley.

Was this a modern receptacle for books? Were ALL those books inside? I found keys with arrows on them and pressed the down arrow until *To Kill a Mockingbird* was selected. The title page of the book appeared. After a few moments, I discovered how to change the page. This was a magical, wonderful...flat library!

I suddenly had trouble catching my breath. Nothing like this had ever happened to me; no one had ever given me such a gift! I existed below the radar of the community, and even my own family. My new cousin sent me a present that was so thoughtful, so personal! She didn't even really know me!

And I could never *let* her know me.

If she ever found out my secret, she would very likely turn away like every single other person in my life. Except for Peter—and occasionally Wee Lilac.

*She must never, ever find out what I am able to do.*

**3**

The rest of Harvest week went quickly because I lost myself in thoughts of what I read the night before and anticipated what I would read that evening. I barely slept, just spent most of the evenings immersed in books!

I got halfway through the third book in the *Twilight* series when the device stopped working. The light turned off, and it wouldn't come back to life no matter how hard I pressed the buttons.

I tried writing a letter to Chrys. I began several notes in my head, but then I was stuck. I didn't know what to say to her other than thanking her for her extraordinary gift. Which no longer worked.

Saturdays were free days. Children played outside, and families visited with one another. Most of my family usually headed to the river with a basket of food and a picnic blanket. I was never invited.

The river was wide and deep, and it was the primary security device for the community. There was a bridge connecting The Outside and The People's Land, with a heavy wooden gate, which was kept locked at all times. The men who were on delivery unlocked it to exit and enter, but it was otherwise permanently closed.

The Outside was about a mile from the edge of the river. The stretch of land between them and us was a dry grass and rock-covered expanse. In the distance, tall buildings were visible. They looked completely unlike any type of building where we lived and were so tall that they pierced the clouds on darker days.

If someone were utterly determined to cross the river into our territory it could happen, but the water rushed quickly around sharp rocks, making any attempt dangerous. A few Outsiders managed to make it across, but they looked so different than The People in the way that they were clothed they were identified immediately and marched out of the gate. Mostly they were just curious about the property. One crossed because of an issued dare. Another was inebriated and didn't really remember why he had made the trip at all.

With the house empty, I decided to do my writing on the porch. The midmorning sun warmed my arms. I removed my gloves since there was no one present to terrify by being bare-handed. I stretched my fingers, running them along the wood beneath me. Picking up my pencil was so much simpler this way, and I enjoyed the stiff, strong feel of it.

*Dear Chrys,*

*I understand why you might want to skip ahead in the book. I took a look at what interested you, and it was interesting to me too. I wish I could spend more time on it, but I feel like we must fully discuss the book of Genesis. You were curious about how God was able to create the world so quickly. He is God, Chrys! He can do anything imaginable (and beyond imagining, too).*

*The next book is Exodus. The People feel very passionately about it because it is about an escape from slavery. We feel like our own Exodus, many years ago, was similar. The Founding Fathers felt that they were becoming slaves to modern immorality. They wanted to create a home where they could concentrate on God and his plans for his sons and daughters. Moses is an important person to us, and we celebrate his bravery.*

*You asked about our name. We are called The People because we are the people who follow God. We are THE People. The rest of humanity are just plain old people. When the city began to grow, the land that we live on became sort of a ghost town. The river was a bit of a divider that didn't seem worth the hassle, I suppose. Our Founding Fathers purchased the land and turned it into The People's Land. It actually got that title because that was just literally what it was. The People's Land.*

*To address your curiosity about the flowers: they are called Opus Dei (God's Work, in Latin), and our land possesses the only soil suited to grow them. You won't find them anywhere else in the world, which serves as proof that our people, our land, is blessed. The girls are all named after flowers to remind us of how unimportant we are, in the whole of God's work. There are countless Daisies, Roses, Lavenders, etc. on the planet. Unlike the Opus Dei, we are common and replaceable. Those other flowers grow naturally on our land, too, and serve as a visual reminder of how dull and fragile we are in comparison to the Opus Dei.*

*Please let me know if you have any questions regarding Exodus. I will do my best to give you the answers you need.*

*It looks like today is going to be a very warm day. I look forward to twilight when things might cool down a bit.*

> *Blessings to you,*
> *Rose of Sharon*

I wondered if my clues were strong enough. I hoped she would look in the back of the book (of course she would, but I just didn't want to take any chances) and find the device there. I prayed that my "twilight" clue would come across as well, because I was desperate to find out what happened to Edward and Bella. The flat library needed to be fixed, but I couldn't even begin to imagine how to do it. Hopefully, a trip to The Outside could provide the required repair.

Standing and dusting off my bottom, I prepared to return to my room to rewrap the gift, insert the letter, and cover the book with its cloth and string. Footsteps crunched along the side of the house, making me pause. Hurrying to slip on my gloves, I tucked the letter under my arm.

Peter stepped out from the side wall; a big grin stretched across his freckled cheeks.

"Hey, Fleur." He lifted an impish eyebrow but had the decency to look around for other listening ears as he said it.

"Peter–" I shook my head.

"What are you doing?" Putting a foot up on the bottom porch step, he leaned in.

"I was writing to my cousin."

For days I had been mulling over the idea of telling him about my miraculous gift. I knew I could trust him. He was probably the only one that I *could* trust. I just didn't want to pass any information along to him that might get him in trouble. If he knew that I had it, and someone found out, he would be considered guilty as well. If it had been a school week I probably wouldn't have been able to keep it from him at all because I was so excited about it at first.

"Can I trust you? I mean really, truly trust you?" I bit my lip, still not entirely convinced that I was making the right choice.

Peter's eyebrows pulled together.

"Yes, of course." He spoke with such intensity that I knew my secret would be safe with him.

"Follow me."

We probably had another hour or two before my

family would return. I was convinced that bringing the device out of my room, out in the open, would be a terrible idea. Bringing Peter into my bedroom was an equally terrible idea. If anyone caught us together in my quarters, I would be beaten. He would be publicly berated. Being together behind the deserted barn was even pushing the rules a bit. Girls and boys were not supposed to be alone together. Since the two of us were largely ignored, no one seemed to care about our time spent in the shadows. My bedroom would be a completely different ball of wax.

Fortunately, the back of the house was generally avoided for fear of running into me.

Opening the door, I beckoned him inside.

"Hurry up!" Grabbing his arm, I pulled him beyond the threshold and slammed the door behind him.

The windowless room was always dark, even during the day. Carefully lighting the lantern, I placed it on my table, realizing how small the space was with his tall body in there with me. Uneasy, Peter moved from foot to foot, as if he stood on a rocking boat.

"Swear to me, Peter, that you will never tell."

Looking intrigued but worried, he used his pointer finger to make a crossing motion over his chest.

I pulled the impossibly tiny collection of reading material from under my pillow. I kept it hidden, sandwiched between my hands. I had last-minute, second thoughts about showing him, but then I made the leap.

"What is it?" Peter asked.

"It's a library."

"What do you mean?" He stepped away, a little frightened by it.

"It's broken or something, right now, so I can't show you. I'm sending it back to Chrys to see if it can be fixed. There are dozens of books inside of it. You turn the pages by pressing these bits on the sides."

"It's amazing. It sort of looks like a larger version of John Junior's phone."

"I thought so, too!" I admitted, pulling the crinkly paper that it came wrapped in out of my desk drawer.

"Wait!" He stopped me from rewrapping it. "Can I touch it?"

Feeling its smooth edges, examining the buttons, even smelling it, he handed it back. When I revealed the missing portion of the Bible, placing it in the carved-out nest, he laughed in disbelief.

"Very clever, isn't she?" Becoming more comfortable in my room, he sat at the desk.

"Yes, I believe so. She has so many questions about where we live. I have questions, too, but I'm so afraid that my letters are being read by Father, or John Junior...one of the Elders, even...I'm trying to talk to her in code, and it seems to be working." I explained how the last letter had led to the receipt of the flat library.

Peter offered to deliver the package to John Junior for me. I had already confided in him about my last visit, and how odd it had been. Hurriedly tucking my letter into the book, I set the device back into its carved-out spot, wrapped it, tied it, and handed it to my friend.

"I think I should probably be going, Fleur. This would look bad if anyone saw us."

I loved the way he had begun exclusively using the name that my mother had chosen for me.

Reaching for the door handle, he turned at the last moment, causing me to bump into his chest. *When had he grown so tall?*

"See you at church tomorrow," he said, stepping out into Saturday afternoon.

Watching him put his hat on and walk away, I felt an almost unbearable loneliness drape over my heart.

# 4

C hurch was the most important event of the week, every week. Almost like a town hall meeting, we were informed of any changes happening within the community: purchases, weddings, deaths, births. We recited passages from the Bible, then the Host Elder explained what we'd just said, adding his own ideas to the mix. Then we sang a multitude of hymns, accompanied by my schoolteacher, who played the piano—the one and only musical instrument allowed on our property. Music, it had often been explained, could lead people to believe that they can create beautiful things that evoke emotions. Only God should be allowed to do this. It was a bit of the which-came-first-the-chicken-or-the-egg conundrum, trying to imagine where the hymns had originated, but no one else seemed troubled by it.

The females sat on the right side of the church. The males sat on the left. Although the church was always crowded, I sat on my own small bench in the back. The women—anyone over the age of 16—had to remain standing throughout the duration of the service, otherwise they might have become too comfortable to truly listen to the lessons we were being taught. This led to quite a lot of fainting, but the tradition continued to stand. Literally.

Men and children could sit for all parts, excluding the hymns. Everyone rose to sing.

Peter was sitting almost directly across from me with the boys and men of his family, so I was able to catch his eye throughout the day. I found warmth and laughter there. His hair had been dutifully slicked down, and he'd found some trousers long enough to cover his ankles. I felt dowdy in comparison, my green rough-hewn, shapeless dress hanging like a large sack from my shoulders. We didn't wear aprons in the chapel, so none of the women looked like they had waists.

The Hawkins women looked like they had recently spent some time on a battlefield: They were slumped in exhaustion, their thin shoulders rounding with tired posture. Intermittently they leaned upon one another for support. One wife had a muslin sling holding her arm close to her chest, and another had a giant purple welt across her forehead. I glimpsed it when she turned to glare in my direction.

An Elder took his place in front of the somber crowd. This week there had been two births, one boy and one girl. An elderly Samuel had died in his sleep. One of the boys had moved into the role of flower delivery.

Trying my hardest to concentrate on the lessons, my

mind kept drifting to the books that I had recently discovered. The little modern library held so many works that Father's did not. I read three Jane Austen novels, *Emma* being my favorite. *Flowers in the Attic*, by V.C. Andrews was terrifying, but I could relate on some level to the unwanted children. The *Twilight* books were lovely, and I couldn't wait to continue with the series. I suddenly realized what was missing from my father's forbidden books: Romance. Not one of them presented a burgeoning relationship from a young woman's point of view. Those new stories made me think about Jasmine and Young Luke, kissing behind the cow barn. I wondered what it would feel like to—

"YOU WILL BE SAVED!" The Host Elder boomed.

"AMEN!" I joined the rest of the congregation in response.

# 5

Relief washed over me when I woke to the beginning of a school week. The Harvest really wore me out this time. Always exhausting, the last round of picking made me feel at least twice my age. Those late nights spent reading Chrys's novels had taken their toll, too.

Sitting at my desk in the back of the room, I nodded along with the rest of the long-haired heads, somehow latching on to some kind of automatic synchronicity. I had not an inkling of what Mr. Adams was droning on and on about. Most likely his old standby "Women are due punishment because Eve's debt must be paid" theory.

Although I looked as though I was wholeheartedly agreeing, hopefully, I was really lost in an internal argument with myself about whether Bella should choose Edward or Jacob.

Peter could tell that I was a little out of it when lunchtime arrived. How could I explain to him what I was thinking? He would never understand.

"Fine. Don't talk to me," he pouted. "Soon I won't have to come here anymore anyway."

That definitely brought me back to earth.

"What?"

"I'll be eighteen very soon. In eight days, in fact. When it happens, I've decided not to continue."

"You're leaving?" My heart sped up with a growing panic.

"Yes. I've decided to join my brothers in delivery."

"But you always said you'd stay..." I couldn't fathom finishing out the year without him.

"You'll be sixteen next month anyway. It's just a couple of months. Then neither one of us will have to come back. Ever." Finally, he looked at me.

A monster was squeezing me from the inside. That was the only explanation for the pain I felt in my chest.

If Peter joined the delivery crew, we would no longer be able to meet behind the barn. I would lose my best friend.

"After school?" he asked, packing away an apple core and his checkered cloth napkin.

I didn't trust myself to speak. I could only nod my head.

Walking back to the classroom didn't have a place in my memory. Sitting at my desk, I couldn't recall the short journey. Mr. Adams was distributing fabric and sewing supplies for our weekly flower sack project. It was part of our duties to create the drawstring bags in which the flowers were transported to The Outside. Hyacinth Small handed a roll of muslin over her shoulder without turning around. I began to thread my needle, putting together two pieces of pre-cut material.

Everyone looked up when the Headmaster entered, beckoning to our teacher.

"I'll be but a moment, ladies," Mr. Adams said, stepping out of the room.

Arms lifted and lowered as they sewed. Girls cast sideways glances around the room, sending looks and gestures to their friends.

Only one girl dared to speak.

"So, Rose of Sharon," Jasmine drawled, enunciating each syllable of my name, "you're pretty lucky to have your own bedroom."

The sewing slowed, but no one looked in my direction.

"I guess it's hard to sleep with those gloves. Is that why they keep you away from everyone else? So, you can take them off?"

I tried my best to let the words just float away. Instead, they floated over and stuck right to me.

"I heard the strangest story about why you have to keep your hands covered," she continued. "I wonder if the story is true?'

Many of the girls stopped sewing altogether.

Jasmine glanced toward the classroom door, standing up to see through the little square window in the middle of it, checking for adults.

She walked over to my desk and placed a flat palm on its surface.

"Is the story true, Shar'n?"

I didn't look up. "I don't know what you're talking about."

I continued with the rhythm of my sewing—needle up, needle down.

"Oh, look," she said, sauntering over to one of the three windows along the wall. "Dead flies. How sad."

She picked up the insect with a thumb and forefinger, then lazily traipsed back to my seat.

"Can you help this fly, Shar'n?"

Two additional girls walked to the windows, gathering more flies. The poor things were constantly dotting the sills after trying to escape through the glass.

"Raise the fly, Shar'n," she commanded, the same smirk on her face that I'd suffered through all of Harvest week.

She flicked the small body in my direction, and it caught my chin, dropping onto the sack that I was trying to make. Soon another one sailed at me. And another. Giggling filled the air.

"Raise the fly! Raise the fly!" the girls began to chant. Soon the chorus sounded as though it came from one source, and fists pounding on various surfaces joined the words.

A pencil flew in my direction, then a wadded-up piece of paper.

Mr. Adams entered as an apple smacked me in the nose with a sickening crunch, the pain making me drop my needle.

"Girls!" In a mere second, they returned to their assigned seating, like it had never happened. Mr. Adams looked in my direction, a scowl hardening his face.

"Rose of Sharon, what is the meaning of this?" Foot tapping angrily, he glared at me, waiting for an answer.

I didn't have one for him, not one that he would approve of anyway.

"I think it best that you go home for the day, young lady." Jabbing his thumb toward the door, as if I didn't understand how to exit the room. "This kind of behavior is unacceptable in the classroom."

There was no point in arguing my innocence. I folded my unfinished project, carefully placing the still-connected needle and spool of thread on top and placed them in my satchel.

On my way out, I paused at Jasmine's desk and calmly stated, "Jasmine, it's so wonderful that you are able to finish your chores in time to spend your afternoons relaxing behind the cow barn with your friend. I truly envy you that."

Bright blue eyes surrounded in thick, black lashes widened in alarm, and Jasmine audibly gasped.

It can feel so wonderful to get the last word in sometimes, can't it?

It felt so good that I forgot to dwell on the surely impending consequences.

## 6

G oing home was not an option for me. The little ones and the wives would have to scramble to improvise an elaborate charade of not noticing how early I returned, but my father would have heard about it immediately. One of the women would run to the blue building, knocking on the door. Even if one of the wives didn't tattle, Mr. Adams would surely inform him, soon enough, and I wished to stretch the calm before the storm out as far as I could. It had been a long time since I'd felt the sting of Father's switch, and I wasn't eager to revisit the sensation. Instead, I sat behind the abandoned barn, choosing to wait until Peter arrived. It would have to be a quick visit so that I could take care of my chore. However, I knew he would be worried about me after hearing about what happened.

Listening to the music of nature around me, I found myself drifting off. The sound of insects and light breeze hummed, lulling me to sleep. I woke to Peter's voice.

"Lord above, Fleur, your eye!" Kneeling before me, he

brushed his fingers gently over the left side of my face.

"Is it bad?" My eye didn't hurt. It was my nose that constantly pulsed in a dull ache.

"You look like you've been in a fight. Or like you're one of John Senior's wives."

Even though it was an unkind joke, it made me laugh.

"One of the girls threw an apple at my face. It was awful, Peter." Tears gathered, though I made a valiant attempt to hold them back.

"I heard about it. I was so worried. I can't believe you were the one sent home for it. Jasmine was the ringleader, wasn't she?" It wasn't a question at all.

I nodded my head. "Peter, I've been thinking. I've decided that I'm glad you're leaving the school. I am just envious."

"Fleur, I don't want to leave you alone. My father…" He looked away.

"It's his decision?"

"Yes. He's always been embarrassed by me, you know. He's the one that added "Sickly" to my name. It's time for me to become a man, I've been informed. I'm to join my brothers in delivery. Then I suppose that's it for me—delivering flowers, getting married, having loads of children, and then dying."

"You make it sound so awful. You've got years before you have to marry anyone, Peter. And you'll get to go to The Outside." I tried to cheer him up.

"Yes, Fleur. I've got years before I have to marry someone. But … you don't."

"What?"

"You don't. You'll be sixteen in a few weeks. You could be married off at any time." He sounded miserable.

"No, no, no. Come on, Peter. Think about it. No one wants to have anything to do with me."

He leaned forward, forcing eye contact.

"I do," he said.

Butterflies danced in my stomach, and I felt my face felt hot. My heart became warm, too, the rhythm of it now suddenly uneven.

He took my hands in his and began to remove my gloves, carefully tugging at the tip of each finger until they slipped away, first the right and then the left, dropping to the ground in a whisper.

Grasping my bare fingers with his large, cool ones, he pulled me against his chest.

When had he become so strong? Why hadn't I noticed? He was *Sickly* Peter. Peter who was always ill, always weak. This Peter was a man, and I completely missed the transformation.

Two lonely children sitting at their own empty lunch tables, we became friends when I was six and he was eight. One day he joined me, laying his buttered bread and strawberries out on the table. We'd eaten together ever since, eventually moving to the ground to escape the stares of those around us.

That was the Peter that I knew. Spending so much time with him, I neglected to see that he had grown up.

"I'm scared, Fleur." He was stronger, maybe, but still

my worried Peter.

"Me, too." I leaned into him, and he wrapped me into a tight embrace. "I think Jasmine is going to try to get back at me."

Leaning away so he could see my face, he asked, "What am I missing here?"

"I was so angry about what happened in class that I told her that I saw her behind the barn. With Luke. I didn't use his name, I just said 'friend,' but she knows now, Peter. She knows."

Peter sighed. "She's probably already made a plan to deal with you. She's not a nice person, Fleur. Please be careful."

I already knew that.

"I need to get home. I have to do my chores." I hated pulling away from him. Picking up my gloves, I stood over him, peering down into his open, familiar face.

"Be careful," he repeated.

I gave the leather at my wrists a final tug, nodding my head.

Retreating toward my house, I left him sitting there.

# 7

The news had already spread. The wives monitored me under hooded eyes, unable to resist the temptation of looking at The Girl Who Would Be Punished. Collecting the fire pit trash, and then depositing it, I returned to the porch for the compost garbage. I dreaded the trip out to the pig pen.

The slop bucket seemed a million times heavier than the last time I'd walked it over to the hungry animals. Cat danced around my heels as I walked, and I feared tripping over him as the bucket banged against my apron, spilling drips over the side.

Dumping the smelly mess into the pig trough, I swatted Cat away from the pigs' nasty dinner. Something looked good to the feline, though, and he couldn't be deterred.

"So," a sugary voice called to me from behind the barn, "you must be pretty brave to come out here all by yourself."

Jasmine and two of her friends stepped from their cover.

"You just stay away from me." I clenched my bucket against my chest, wondering if it would be an effective weapon against three people.

"Oh, don't worry," she purred, "we'll stay away from you. We've been warned our whole lives to do just that." Her companions snickered.

Dropping the bucket, I yanked my right hand free of its cover, realizing the best way to deal with the bullies. Holding my hand up high, I stepped toward them, reaching.

"Want to see what this can do? Huh?"

All three cringed and jumped away. I wiggled my fingers toward their faces.

"Want to see if the stories are true?" Taking another step in their direction, I forced myself to smile. "There's only one way to find out, right?"

"You–you stay away from us!" Jasmine was satisfyingly terrified, as were her companions.

"Sure, Jasmine. I was just leaving." Reaching down for the bucket, I tucked the empty glove into the waistband of my apron, lifting Cat. Picking him up under his stomach, I tore him away from the pigs' meal.

"See you, later," I called to them, not turning around as I left.

"I'm not done with you yet, Shar'n!" Jasmine screeched with a snarl.

Hurrying home, I found the front yard empty. Everyone was inside. Because I completed my chores later than usual, I missed dinner. There wasn't a plate or bowl waiting on the porch, like there usually was.

*Was starvation part of my punishment?*

Dropping the bucket in its place on the side of the house, I rounded the corner to my room. The door was propped open.

Father was sitting on my bed, switch in hand. His face was eerily pale in the darkness. The lantern sat cold and unused on my desk.

"Father." My teeth chattered.

"Rose of Sharon." As always, he avoided my eyes, focusing on my nose. His glance flickered up to my black eye, although his expression didn't change.

"It wasn't my fault, Father. They threw things at me. They hurt me."

"Mr. Adams said—"

"He wasn't even in the room, Father! *I did nothing wrong.* Nothing."

"You expect me to believe you, and not your teacher." He shifted a bit in his seat.

"Please, Father. *Please.*" I whispered, desperate.

"Put your hands on the wall, please," he ordered. He could have been requesting another serving of potatoes at the dinner table. Or asking a neighbor if he could borrow a tool.

I did as I was told, turning to face the wall, placing one bare hand and one covered hand up on the flat surface. I closed my eyes.

My last whipping happened years ago, just after I

began going to school. I don't remember what I had done to deserve it, but I had never forgotten the pain.

This was so much worse.

The rule was one lashing per year of life. If all this occurred eighteen days from now, I would have received sixteen lashes. I guess I got off easy.

Most of the sharp flicks landed on my bottom and my calves, but my back did not come away unscathed. He didn't tell me to turn when he was finished, but I heard him leave the room and close the door, leaving me in darkness. I collapsed to the floor, sobs heaving from the pit of my stomach. The pain of the welts on my behind complained loudly.

I rose to my knees, felt around for my wooden matchbox and managed to light one of the matches. The lantern glowed with a warm light, but I felt so cold.

On my bed was a familiar-shaped package.

Impossible.

Father had beaten me, yet let me have my cousin's delivery? Unfathomable!

Lying on the bed, I shifted to my side to avoid the painful pressure on my back.

Once uncovered, the Bible looked as it always had, of course. The expected sheet of stark paper sat inside the cover, but I didn't read it. I hurriedly flipped to the back of the book, to the secret compartment. My library had returned!

I unwrapped it and found another small square of yellow paper affixed to its screen:

"I like the *Twilight* books, too! Team Edward? Or Team Jacob?"

Another tiny bundle, also wrapped in the soft, crinkly paper, was wedged underneath where the device had sat. In wonder, I pulled the paper free.

Was it a telephone? John Junior was the only person I'd ever seen with a telephone. It was constantly up against his ear as he traveled about. It was his lifeline to The Outside, and all the Opus Dei orders that came in. I had never seen the telephone up close.

This device was much smaller than John Junior's telephone, though. It was a small silver square, with buttons forming a circle. There was a black wire plugged into it and wrapped around the device. There were two little balls at the ends of the wires.

Was it a game of some sort? A video game like those that I'd read about in some of Father's books? I pressed the buttons to see what would happen.

After pressing the button with a rectangle on it, noises came out through the little balls at the end of the wire. I held them up to my face, then realized that they would fit into my ears.

Music like nothing I had ever heard filled my head. Instruments that I couldn't name and didn't know existed played around a heavenly male voice. He sang of love and loss. Like the library, this little piece of plastic seemed to hold many songs. The beauty of it all held me frozen in place. Listening. Listening. Listening.

I attempted to read Chrys's note, but the sounds were

too distracting. This music was nothing like the hymns from church. It was…complicated. So many sounds, so much feeling and emotion! I pulled the balls out of my ears. I could still hear the songs quietly playing, but it wasn't quite so overwhelming.

*Dear Rose of Sharon,*

*Exodus was intriguing. I can't believe that the Pharaoh wanted to kill all those babies! And how ironic that Moses was raised in his home. Pretty cool. I knew there were ten commandments, but not what they were. Good rules, all of them, I guess. My mom probably likes the "Thou Shalt Honor Thy Mother and Father" one the best, although she'd change it to just "Honor Thy Mother" if she could, I'll bet. See the pages if you want to see my notes.*

*I'm going to go out on a limb, and guess that Leviticus is next. I'll take a look, as soon as possible. It must feel powerful being a teacher of religion. Be sure to send the Bible back when you feel like you need a new burst of power.*

*Thank you for doing this!*
*Chrys*

"A new burst of power." I laughed aloud. My cousin was pretty good at writing in code as well!

The pain from Father's switch and the hunger from lack of dinner felt miles away as I found the page that I'd been reading when the power ran out.

*Team Edward, definitely.*

# 8

My dream was real. It was a dream, but its progression was identical to what had transpired in the past. And instead of being in it, I was forced to watch it, forced to view things that I did and that had happened to me.

Not even in school, yet—I was just a year younger than Wee Lilac.

And the flowers were dying.

All four fields of Opus Dei had steadily wilted throughout the week. Collapsed flowers covered the soil, overlapping one another in a sad rug of decay. The palette had dimmed spots of brown covering their shriveled petals, thousands of blooms dead.

Sitting on Father's strong hip with my arms wrapped around his neck, I listened to the conversation he was having with three men in white coats. They were the men from the blue building who studied the flowers. The Elders were all there, too.

Father brought me with him because he liked me to be his companion everywhere we went when he wasn't working at the office. Grandmother usually watched me because the other one who used to take care of me was gone now. Father said I was his partner and he liked having me around.

"What can be done?" one of the Elders asked, his tone unbearably sorrowful.

"There is no way to figure out how this has happened. We're trying, but we keep hitting a brick wall." This was from one of the men in the white coats.

"This is going to hurt us very badly, financially," Father stated, his mouth cemented in a deeper frown than usual.

"We know that, Joseph. I mean, look at this!" the Elder spun around, arms open, gesturing to the four pitiful fields. "It's going to take weeks to replant all of this!"

They spoke amongst themselves with concerned voices as I shimmied down Father's leg.

"I can help!" No one heard me. They were too busy arguing in their deep male voices.

"Papa! I can help!" I made a ring around my mouth with little cupped hands and yelled up at him.

"Not right now, Rose of Sharon." Barely casting a glance in my direction, he buried his hands in his pockets, listening to the Elders lament the current turn of events.

"I'll fix you," I earnestly promised to the field in front of me, squatting and wrapping my fingers around the stem of the first drooped flower of the first row.

Whispers filled my brain. Words. Many I didn't understand.

The buzz in my fingertips licked its way to my palms, spreading to my wrists. The head of the flower lay across the one next to it, and I could feel the tingling extend from one bloom to the next, slowly building momentum.

The first Opus Dei's stem regained its healthy green glow. The petals slowly filling with color, the flower standing itself up tall and proud—then the next, and the next. One after the other they lifted, thoroughly rejuvenated. The motion zig-zagged through the plot of land, back and forth along the row, like a game of dominoes with the tiles knocking each other down in a spill, but this was in reverse, and in resplendent technicolor.

Each flower seemed to comfort the next, the color crawling up from the soil, reaching the round head, then spreading to its neighbor.

"Great God above." The men turned to witness the unlikely miracle.

"What is happening?" This one sounded frightened.

"It's the girl! She's a witch!"

"What is this child, Dark Joseph? Is she a demon? What unholy power is this?" an elder demanded, shouting at my father.

The field was finally resurrected, the brilliant rainbow vivid and very much alive, and I turned to my audience.

"It's the seeds," I explained. "They said the seeds were bad."

Father gaped at me. The others backed away, terrified.

"We must not speak of this."

"This is the work of the Devil."

"She is an abomination."

I thought I had helped them, and now they hated me. I didn't understand.

Without speaking, Father lifted me with his strong hands around my small waist, keeping his arms outstretched, and walked us home in a hurry.

Still not offering any words, Father sat me on a chair in the kitchen and disappeared into his bedroom, reappearing with heavy woolen mittens.

"Do not ever remove these from your hands. Do you hear me?"

I nodded my head, tears dripping onto my lap.

"I thought I was helping, Papa."

He didn't answer me.

\*\*\*

I woke with a moan.

Abruptly, I remembered my aunt and Chrys. The memories flooded my whole being; smells, tastes, and sounds all flooding through my brain at a fantastic speed.

My aunt was called Iris. She was beautiful, and people would always say that she bore more than a passing resemblance to my mother. Chrysanthemum and her mom watched me at our house during the day while Father worked. Every so often, Aunt Iris would be gone to Harvest, and my cousin and I would spend time with my grandmother. But most of the time she took care of us.

Aunt Iris would bake with us, letting our little dimpled hands roll the dough. She played games with us and sang songs that we never heard on Sundays. Sometimes we would watch her write stories, the pencil flying across the paper on our dining table.

"Remember," she would say, raising a finger to her lips. *No telling.*

Once Father returned from the blue building in the evening, tired and distant, my beloved aunt and cousin would walk down the street to that big house with a wraparound porch.

It was plain to see, even at my age, that my father was still mourning my mother.

I recalled a day when I found a baby bird beneath our big tree in the yard. The poor thing had fallen from the nest, and life was swiftly draining from its tiny, feathered body. When it no longer moved after shuddering from the shock of impact, I wrapped my hands around it, squeezing gently. After it completed the reanimation process in my cupped palms, I released it onto the grass.

Iris had been watching.

"She fell. She said she wanted her mama," I interpreted sagely, owning more words than should belong to a child of less than three.

"You can't do things like that, Rose of Sharon. *You must never let anyone see you do anything like that,* okay?" When I didn't answer right away, she shook me, so I nodded my head.

I decided to only help ladybugs, other insects, and small creatures when no one was around. Bringing the dead back to life drained all my energy away, but it was a good tired, like the cathartic feeling one gets after a long cry. The exhaustion never lasted more than a few hours. The tremendous feeling of aiding someone who needed help coming back never, ever went away.

Then suddenly my aunt and cousin were gone.

Grandmother took care of me after that. She wasn't blatantly unkind, but I never felt the warmth and joy that radiated from Aunt Iris. Sometimes she would talk about my mother, and the things she told me weren't always positive.

"She had strange ways, from growing up on The Outside."

"She stole my son from any of the decent girls who were raised with The People."

"Your mother sometimes acted in ways that we do not approve."

Even though I could sense the distaste in her statements, I loved hearing anything I could about the woman who birthed me. Father never said a single word about her.

After the day at the field when I revived the blooms, Grandmother would never again let me near her. She wouldn't look at me, wouldn't speak to me. If I got too close, she would scoot away and didn't even try to hide it.

Soon, I began to notice that *all* people avoided me. When children tried to be friendly, their parents would drag them to safety. Later, the wives began appearing, and it was my own family who treated me like a ghost.

After the first baby was born, Father built my room on the back of the house. That wife wanted no chance of what I could do corrupting or harming her precious child. Cutting and hammering for over a week, wiping his face with a handkerchief, father erected the dark little addition to the home that was once my haven. Now I was barely allowed inside.

I missed Aunt Iris and her daughter for quite a long time, and then, as happens with childhood memories, they disappeared from my past. All that remained was a tiny glimmer when someone said or did something that reminded me of my time with them. "That seems so familiar," I would think.

But I never knew why.

# 9

This Harvest week felt like every other Harvest week. The power ran out of my magic library by Tuesday, so I didn't have anything to look forward to and the hours limped by. By Wednesday, I realized that Peter's birthday was the following morning and I would never sit with him at lunch, ever again. Melancholy limited my movements, making my chores take longer than ever. I couldn't light a fire under the cauldron. I forgot the lye in the first batch. When I tried to pin things up to dry, I kept dropping them in the dust, and had to rewash them.

I finally crawled into bed after eleven o'clock, forcing Cat to lie with me so I had something to hold on to. I couldn't sleep. Even after hours of physical labor, knowing I had to wake early to take down the underclothes and sort them, I still couldn't sleep. Cat, however, draped across my shoulders and snored. His fur tickled my chin.

Carefully, I lifted the ball of fluff off of me and placed him on my pillow. I found a sheet of paper in my drawer, noting that I was running low, and began to write.

> *Dear Chrys,*
>
> *I do need to feel the charge of power that I get from contacting you. In fact, I feel that I need it doubly, this time.*
>
> (The music maker had also stopped working.)
>
> *Much of Leviticus is about sacrifice and atonement. I am interested to hear what you think about it. More about Moses, too. I am especially interested in continuing our lessons, since I will soon no longer attend school. I will be sixteen in less than two weeks. Since the school year is almost over, I will remain a student. However, following this summer I will no longer be able to attend. These letters will keep me practiced in reading and writing.*
>
> *Peace be with you,*
> *Rose of Sharon*

I prepared the package, placing it on my desk for the morning.

And still, I couldn't find slumber. Restless, I obsessively continued to ponder how I may never again be able to visit with Peter behind the abandoned barn. He would be one of the men on delivery now. I might only see him peeking out from the back of a wagon, on his way to The Outside.

Anxious and fidgety, I wandered outside to see if the

laundry had dried. Most of it was ready to be taken down, and I placed it in the proper basket. By the time I was finished, the rest was dry too.

Morning sounds began to emanate from the house: women waking, preparing for another day of picking flowers, buckets filling over and over and over again in the sweltering near-summer blaze.

After I readied for the day, I decided to deliver the book to John Junior. Quickly packing a lunch, I grabbed the package and headed to his house.

Once again, a woman answered the door. Her eyes turned to slits when she recognized me, and she pulled her body away. John Senior quickly joined her.

"Ahhh, dear Rose of Shar'n. Another bit of mail to send with my boy?" He pushed the door fully open and waved his wife behind him, joining me on the porch.

"Yes, Sir."

"Ye don't need to call me 'Sir', my girl. Ye can call me 'John.'" Decaying teeth flashed beneath that yellowing brush of facial hair, just before he was swallowed by a coughing fit. Pulling a handkerchief from his pocket, he lifted a finger, telling me to wait.

John Junior joined us, coming from around the back of the house.

"Hello, Rose of Sharon," he greeted.

"Hello." I shyly handed him my bundle, and he accepted it.

"I'm just about to head to The Outside, so you've got pretty good timing." He smiled a genuine, not-rotten smile.

"That's my boy," John Senior drawled, "always on *The Outside.*"

There was some hidden meaning in the words, an inside joke or story shared by the two men. It was lost on me, though.

"Well, thank you." I nodded at them both, taking a step off of the porch.

"Have fun pickin', today, dear," John Senior called, turning again to cough.

Clutching my lunch bag, I hustled to the field.

# 10

J asmine kept her distance all week. I sometimes saw her during our lunch break, but she never looked for me. Always surrounded by other girls, she had a nice ring of human insulation.

By Thursday I was able to harness a jolt of energy, knowing that the week was almost finished. The Field Master let me be too. I kept my head down, did my job, and returned home to finish my chores.

When the Field Master blew his whistle to signify the end of the working day, I gathered my lunch bag and walked along the dirt road along with the other females. Many of them linked arms with a friend or sibling or walked together in small groups. As always, I walked alone.

Sitting on the porch steps, I ate my stew in silence, still wincing at the pain on my bottom. I left the empty bowl and gathered the metal pail to fill with slops for the pigs.

My relatives continued to eat at the dinner table,

purposely not registering that I was in the kitchen gathering the food trash from under the metal sink. Wee Lilac turned her head ever so slightly and winked.

*Maybe Jacob deserved a second chance*, I thought. My *Twilight* obsession had begun to border on being unhealthy. Before the library died on me, I had begun to read *Divergent*. I almost hoped my brain would soak in the story, allowing me to turn *Twilight* loose.

The moon shone like a sharp, thin crescent. Everything was drenched in dark shadow, but there was enough light for me to find my target, and I leaned over the outside of the pig pen to pour the pungent soup of leftovers into the rectangular wooden trench.

"Come and get it, piggies!" I called. They didn't need to be asked twice!

My inquisitiveness would not allow me to walk away without checking the rear of the cow barn. I *had* to know if she was back there, reckless as it seemed. As I did the first time, I leaned my back against the stiff wall and slid my body until I reached the sharp intersection.

Bending at the knees, I twisted my waist to peer at the land behind the barn.

No Jasmine. No Luke.

But there was something on the damp grass, a small mass where I once spied the lovers.

Approaching the mystery lump, I dropped the bucket. The diminutive moon did little to help me identify the dark bulge nestled in the turf.

It was Cat. My pet was bunched up in the fetal

position, head at a peculiar angle. His tongue lolled, as if he wanted to taste the ground beneath him.

"No!" I wailed.

First Peter was leaving me, now Cat.

"No, Cat, no!"

I ripped my gloves away, wrapping my fingers around my furry friend, lifting him to my bosom.

*She did this to me. The mean one. She broke my neck...*

The fizzle climbed to my palms but couldn't transfer to the animal.

"Please, God, *please!*" I sobbed.

It was faint, but it was there. The transfer of life, of power. The distinctive murmur of vitality shifted from my body to the cat's.

The drain on my soul was nearly intolerable. Breath could not fill my lungs, and I fell to my knees, suffocating.

Finally, the animal twisted from my arms, turning to look at me, offering me thanks with his strange, glowing green eyes.

"Thank you!" I choked, looking to the heavens. "Thank you, God."

I forgot to bring the bucket, wrapping my arms around Cat, determined to bring him home.

Our yard was filled with people when we arrived. All my sisters were there: Calla, Tulip, Blonde Lilac, Azalea, Bluebell Quick, Wee Lilac, Camellia. And my brothers: Ezekiel, Caleb, Benjamin, Eli, Dark David, Abel, Solomon, and Pale Gideon.

The wives stood along the front porch: Orchid,

Delphine, Mother Camellia, Magnolia, and Baker Poppy.

Father and a smattering of men and boys from the community rounded out the crowd. In the center of the group stood Jasmine, and she pointed at me as I approached.

"Do you see?" she screeched. "The animal was dead, but now it lives! I saw it lying dead behind the barn with my very own eyes."

A collective gasp rose from the lawn.

"She is a demon! An unholy witch! She brought that cat back from the dead!"

That clever girl finally found a way to get back at me. She had set me set up! Jasmine knew that I would be near the barn, and that I would look behind it.

Someone screamed, a murderous siren. The group was a frozen mass for a moment, then they began to gesture and talk animatedly. I dropped Cat and ran, my feet kicking dust into the air.

Where to go? To the only human being that truly cared for me, the only one that I could trust: Peter.

I had never been inside Peter's house, but I knew exactly where it sat—along the bank of tall rocks about a quarter mile from the school. I passed it at least a thousand times throughout the years, sometimes with Peter himself. The house was nice enough, with a small porch, a small garden, and a large front door.

Hysterical, I pounded on the door with both fists.

"Peter!" I cried, "Please let me in!"

Rustling could be heard from within. After seconds

that felt like hours, the door creaked open, revealing my most favorite form. My Peter.

"They're going to kill me, Peter!" I heaved. "I need somewhere to hide!"

A muscled arm appeared above his head, latching onto the top of the door frame. Peter's father, Lemuel, leaned over his shoulder.

"You know this girl, Sickly Peter?" Lemuel's gaze was cold, knowing. With sharp, dangerous focus, he regarded me from head to heel.

Peter's eyes roved, pausing on everything but me, shifting nervously about his yard.

"I'm sorry," Peter exclaimed, "I'm afraid I can't help you."

With that, he closed the door.

My limbs turned into noodles, pooling in front of the large door.

Cries issued from my home's direction. Although I wished to perish there, on the rough wooden boards, I managed to pick myself up and spirit away to the abandoned barn. Collapsing against the wall that I'd leaned against hundreds of times with Peter, I finally caught my frenzied breath.

Was this the end of me? I expected a mob to come, armed with a thick rope twisted into the shape of my neck, ready for a lynching. Every little noise seemed to me an approaching group bent on violence aimed in my direction. The riffling of leaves assumed the sound of an angry mob's footsteps. The breeze was a whisper, calling, "Here she is.

Finally, we've found her."

At least an hour passed, and I was still alive. Crickets chirped, and my bare legs grew cold against the ground.

"Fleur," a familiar tongue called. Peter stepped out of the brush.

Fresh hurt drenched my heart. He had denied me. My Peter had sent me to the wolves.

"I...I am so sorry," he professed, rubbing his uncovered hair. "If you knew my father, you would—"

"Peter, I needed help and you turned me away." My words were like a massive stone wall, standing tall and impenetrable between us.

"Fleur, my father...I don't expect you to forgive me, but he—" Peter slid down the barn wall, landing on the damp ground beside me.

A blue bruise blossomed above his right eyebrow. Miserably, he hung his shaggy head.

"He beats you, doesn't he?" I asked.

"Yes, Fleur, of course he does. I wanted to help you, honest. I just couldn't."

"I understand." My forgiveness sounded foreign to my ears, as though maybe I didn't fully believe what I was saying.

"Thank you, Fleur."

We sat in quietude for a long stretch.

"Fleur, I want to marry you." Peter looked straight ahead, not turning toward my body.

"The Lord knows that no one else does," I joked. Secretly, I thrilled at the idea of becoming his wife.

"I'm serious."

Time passed. Peter held my hands, and the gloves had never felt more like a prison.

"Did you know that they have an apartment?" he asked.

"What?"

"The delivery crew. They have an apartment on The Outside. My brothers say they order pizza and play video games, and they've got computers and television. Some of them have girlfriends."

Of course, I knew the last part. That's how my father met my mother, on one of the delivery visits.

"I don't want to ever find a girlfriend, Fleur. You are the only person for me. I want to grow old with you. I want to give you children." He paused, unsure if he might be overstepping a boundary.

"Oh, Peter," I sighed.

"I love you, Fleur."

Peter put a hand under my chin, his strong hand turning my head to meet his gaze. He was so different from Father, who avoided my eyes like they might burn him to the ground.

He kissed me.

Nothing I had ever read prepared me for the physical reaction my body yielded. My psyche escaped above to the sky above me, landing somewhere among the twinkling stars.

I startled myself by saying the words that I had always known, but had never spoken out loud, "And I love you."

"Listen to me now, Fleur," Peter commanded. "They all believe her. They all believe that Jasmine is telling the truth. But no one will admit it, because they're too afraid, and they don't know what to do with you. I think you will be safe if you pretend that nothing has changed. Just go about your business, and I don't think anyone will question you."

Draping his arm around my shoulder, he pulled me into his body.

"Please," he begged, "please be safe."

The next kiss was more exquisite than my imagination could have possibly allowed. Peter's soft lips covered mine, seeking for *something*. I clung to him, looking for the same. The feeling of his warm mouth pressed along my throat, resting on my collarbone, turned my insides to jelly.

"I have to go now, Fleur, and it might be a long time until I see you again." A tear leaked from his eye, carving a trail toward the lips that had covered mine not minutes before.

"Happy birthday, Peter," I said.

And he was gone.

## 11

Peter was mostly correct about the community's reaction to Jasmine's accusation. I wasn't hunted down and burned at the stake, although my siblings ran from the yard as I approached, and people seemed to put even more distance between us than before.

Apprehensive, I arrived for Friday's shift in the field, but the Field Master merely pointed me away. I picked up my lunch and hid in my room until all lights in the house had been extinguished. No one came out to berate me for not removing the garbage from the house, nor did they leave any dinner for me out front when the sun began to dip behind the tall buildings in the far distance.

Once the family headed to the river on Saturday, I moved out to my spot behind the abandoned barn. I picked through Father's library before I left, taking a crime novel and a couple of muffins from the kitchen along with me. On Sunday I stood at the rear of the church. The congregation cast a wide variety of stares in my direction;

fear, curiosity, and hate among them.

My desk at school mysteriously found a new position at the back of the classroom. I used to have my own row, now I had my own whole section.

The People didn't celebrate birthdays like many do in the world. We didn't bake cakes or wrap presents or sing festive songs. Important birthdays were marked events: At five you earned a spot at the school. If you were a girl, sixteen meant you were eligible for marriage. Boys could leave school the day they turned eighteen.

My birthday was no different than any other day.

I was sixteen now, but it meant almost nothing. School wasn't out for another month, and obviously I had no fiancé waiting eagerly for my change in age. The week plodded along in a wretched, languid fashion. Without Peter there to meet for lunch, one minute seemed to contain a thousand hours.

The only attention I received on the anniversary of my birth was an attempt at tripping me, by one of Jasmine's friends. Gracefully stretching her toe across the aisle as I retreated to my corner to eat, she caught my ankle. Stumbling, I grasped her table, and not anticipating the effect of her cruel action, she shrieked.

"Don't bother, Azalea," Jasmine sneered, "she's not worth it." The girls guffawed most unlady-like in answer.

Mr. Adams must have recycled his lesson plans every few weeks. I had undoubtedly obtained the knowledge he was attempting to distribute at least a half-dozen times in the nearly three years that he led our class. Repeating after the Elder evoked no feeling whatsoever. After so many reminders, I had become desensitized. *Yes, we are evil. We, women, are a distraction, and the embodiment of sin.* It was a wonder that they kept us around! Of course, the men wouldn't have been able to produce offspring without us, and for some reason they were totally against harvesting the Opus Dei with their own hands.

Although Mr. Adams hadn't left our class unattended too many times in the past, he never would again. He purposely kept his steady gaze on his pupils, not even allowing his toe to cross the threshold leading to the outside hallway because of what had happened the last time he'd left us alone.

I suppose he was concerned that I might request more dead flies and fruit be thrown at me. He couldn't allow that, now, could he?

# 12

Although June was quickly approaching, an unlikely rainstorm visited our fields, making Wednesday of Harvest week a muddy affair. The precipitation drenched us within moments of our arrival, our sodden leather shoes rubbing angry blisters onto our frozen feet.

We were required to pick all through the year, so we had dealt with storms before, but this storm gave no warning. When we were prepared, we brought umbrellas. Although picking with only one hand wasn't the most convenient thing to do, it beat the chill of constant drizzle.

Because this downpour was unexpected, by lunch break the women looked like soggy clones huddled beneath the only cover available, an old, gnarled tree on the outskirts of the field. Dripping hair, muddy hems and legs, and lots of shuddering and chattering filled the afternoon.

Buckets weren't filled as quickly as the Field Master preferred, so he strode between rows, screaming into cold ears. Curiously, he kept his distance from my marshy row, castigating the rest of his female crew instead. Another fabulous perk of being given the identity of unholy, satanic witch.

Marching home in the pitch-dark gloomy mist, I shouldn't have been surprised when a thick glob of ooze trickled down the back of my neck. The anonymity of night's dark mask gave the girls behind me a boost of terrible bravery. Keeping my chin held high, I muddled along without even a stumble as wads and clumps connected with my back, head, and rear. I did not doubt for a second that Jasmine was within their ranks.

Following Father's wives and daughters who were old enough to harvest onto our property, I finished the journey at my bedroom door, covered from head to toe in stinging mire.

I couldn't enter like that. I was a poisoned cake covered in nasty frosting.

A complicated routine was played out on the porch as females shucked their ruined clothing. They were being sheltered by, and then covered in, blankets by those who had already completed the process. I imagined them all sitting along the hallway, waiting for their turn in the tub.

When the last had entered the building and dresses were hanging on the line to be showered by God, I stepped up to the pump. I removed my apron, then my gown, and stood amidst the storm in my underclothes. Even my camisole and bloomers had become sodden, the muck seeping through the outer layers.

Once my hair was as clean as I could have hoped, I

scrubbed along my arms, legs, and bare feet. I couldn't figure out how to keep my feet from stepping in the mud, so I just let them remain covered in grimy slippers. Hanging my clothing along the line, I kept it a respectful distance from the ghostly queue of twisting, shapeless gowns and aprons being blown by the wind.

The darkness of my room mirrored the darkness outside, though the dryness was welcome. My fingers shook so violently that I wasted a match, watching it burn to a nub before I was able to light my lantern.

Stepping out of my underclothes, I squeezed the water out of them, reaching my arms out of a crack in the door to do so. The hateful gloves were so much more reviled when soaked against my fingers. Minutes passed before I was able to roll them off, also squeezing them free of the damp.

I'd never been given pajamas. I had one additional dress, which I pulled onto my body, hanging the soggy underclothes across my chair, praying they would dry by morning. There was no hope that the gloves would dry. The skin beneath would remain shriveled throughout the following day, possibly causing the tender, unexposed flesh to blister and peel away.

As the light beneath the glass grew brighter, I felt my spirits rise. On the floor next to the bed was Chrys's Bible.

It had been unwrapped, the muslin underneath it flayed away by someone else's exploring hands. Panicking, I lifted the heavy book and turned to the back. The secret chamber was empty, nothing remaining but the funny, crinkly paper. My heart was broken.

The gift had been stolen, though the usual note remained.

*Hello Rose of Sharon!*

*Leviticus: Whew! What a story. I left some notes along the chapter for you. I'd like to know what you have to say about Azazel, and all those dead goats.*

*Sorry it took so long to respond. I couldn't find the guy who brings the mail for The People. When you get this, you'll know that I finally found him out there, making deliveries.*

*By the way, those flowers you guys grow are HUGE.*

*Looking forward to hearing from you. I'm ready to start reading about Numbers. Is it really about, you know, numbers??? Can we skip that one?*

> *Your Cousin,*
> *Chrys*

There wasn't even any way to figure out if she were sending me any clues, because whatever she would have been getting at was gone.

*Who took my things?* Whoever they were, they now knew enough to condemn me to horrible punishment. I began to shiver, and this time it wasn't from the cold.

*Who?*

At one time I had imagined that it would all be worth whatever kind of discipline could be doled out if I were caught. In the alarming trepidation of reality, I could no longer think those carefree words with any measure of truth. And not knowing the identity of the vandal only made it worse.

Rapid scratching at my door pulled me out of my alarmed reverie. It was Cat, asking to escape from the bluster. Using an extra blanket kept folded at the foot of my bed, I toweled him off, pulling him to my chest for warmth.

As unimaginable as it seemed, I drifted off into a restless sleep with the lantern still blazing. Cat slept, too, purring against my desperately pounding heart.

My last thought before slumber: *too much rain for laundry, so at least I don't have to act as the Underclothes Fairy on this wet, wet Wednesday...*

Thank God for small mercies.

## 13

The sound of Cat's pitiful mews opened my eyes. My head pounded, and my chest felt like a lion sat upon it instead of my skinny pet. Turning my head, I coughed into my pillow, lifting a hand that felt as though it was made of heavy stone to cover my mouth.

Sweat moistened my brow, the sides of my face dripping with it, and still I was made of ice. The pile of rough blankets on top of me vibrated with chills that wouldn't seize.

"I'm sorry, Cat–" I coughed again, unable to continue.

*Water.* I needed water. Thirst made my eyes close tight. A foreign tongue crowded my mouth, swollen, twice the size of my old one. Why was someone else's tongue in my mouth?

*Where is my tongue?* I thought, delirious.

I slept again, just on the edge of being aware of my gratefulness for the peace of unconsciousness.

Hours passed (or just minutes? Days?) before I could

force my eyelids to peel away from one another. Human voices burbled around my head, though I couldn't translate the words.

Father was there, and with him, John Junior.

"–Field Master found you absent, he sent for me."

"–Joseph. If she doesn't drink some water, and...other help, she might not make it. I've always found it so stupid that they make them Harvest when–"

The words fluttered around like wings, some of them too low to hear.

"Drink, Rose of Sharon," Father commanded. Holding water to my lips, he kept the glass steady as I gulped. Much of it escaped from the sides of the glass.

John Junior was absent. Then he returned. I had no way to tell how long his absence lasted, but Father remained sitting on the edge of my bed for the duration.

"Was it you?" I tried to make it sound normal, but all that came out was fuzzy moans.

"What did you say, Rose of Sharon?" Concern seemed to turn my Father's face into another human being, one that I vaguely remembered from years ago.

"The Bible. You took it out, my gift." There. It didn't sound quite like my voice, but the words were recognizable.

He did not speak. Turning his head away, he answered by staring at a wall that had nothing interesting about it to capture his attention.

Finally, John Junior returned, pulling an orange plastic container out of his pocket. It had a typed label around it and looked like it must have come from The Outside. John Junior pressed down on the white lid with his palm, twisting it open.

"You have to swallow these, Shar'n," Father spoke earnestly. Holding two little white circles in his hand, I allowed him to deposit them in my mouth, followed by a trickle of water from the glass.

"You'll have to come back to give her more, Joseph. In about six hours, or this won't really do any good. The fever is too high." Father looked me over, his examination hesitating at my still, naked hands.

"Yes, of course," Father promised, standing.

No other communication was exchanged, and the two men left my small room, once Father had extinguished my lantern. Cat followed along behind them.

My brain attempted to make some sense of it all, but gave up fairly quickly, fading back into comfortable oblivion.

My eyes remained sealed no matter how much effort I lent to opening them.

Time passed, and I realized with a sense of unexpected relief that I must be dead. Then I heard Father enter. His heavy footsteps had become identifiable, familiar. Also, he carried with him a unique scent. Smells from the blue building, maybe? More pills were forced between my lips, my throat reflexively swallowing them, chased by water. Something else flowed as well, a salty broth, warming my insides. I could see nothing behind my firmly locked lids, but could sense a visitor from time to time, knowing without a doubt that it was always my father.

There was more drifting and floating along clouds of darkness. Nestled within giant hands, maybe God's, I sensed a presence.

"Fleur," a woman's voice sang, "you must remain. You must stay with them. You cannot join us yet."

The love encompassed in the voice filled me with hope. It was a feeling that I had never known. True, unburdened love and tender compassion so complete that salty drops escaped from my closed eyelids, coursing along my fevered cheeks.

Feeling returned to my earthly legs and arms.

"No!" I wished to call, but the word was trapped inside. I wanted to remain with this soothing force. Forever.

"Please!"

But now my eyes were open.

## 14

*H* *ungry.*

The rumble in my stomach was rude and persistent. Gathering a deep breath, the sour stench of illness crowded my senses. The blankets surrounding me were thick, crunchy, and odorous. I attempted to stand, a laundry session forefront in my mind. It proved fruitless. My traitorous knees quivered, sending me to the floor.

There I sat for God-only-knows-how-long, when one of the wives, called Magnolia for being born with a nearly white head of hair, appeared in my doorway.

Glaring at me, she surveyed my living area. In her arms, a pile of clean clothes was clenched. Her face twisted in a knot of hate and disgust. Perhaps her animosity was fed by underclothes duty? Had she inherited my chores?

Pointing to the corner, she waved her hand; communication without vocalization the primary goal. Barely able to lift myself into a standing position, I lurched in the assigned direction, leaning in a crouch. Magnolia handed me a napkin, wrapped around a toasted piece of bread. Swallowing it in three bites, I felt almost uncomfortably full. My stomach had shrunk during my illness.

Magnolia cleared the soiled linens and blankets, pinching her face into a visage of disgust. She left the room once she made the bed up with the clean sheets, but first she uttered one word: "Bath."

Using the house as a crutch, I crawled around to the front porch by leaning along the thick boards. If a child or wife spied my broken-down form, they cleared away to who-knows-where. *Poof*, like magic.

The small mirror above the communal little sink bespoke a near trip to lights-out for the girl in the reflection. A shade of grey tinged my features like charcoal. Gripping the edges of the bowl, I was nearly unable to support my weight. I dropped my clean clothes on the floor and began to fill the tub. Steam rose above the water, beckoning me to slip within its waters.

The nubby dress draped over my emaciated form smelled horrible. Peeling it away, I climbed into the tub, feeling warm for the first time since the rain began to fall upon us on Harvest day.

Hearing family business among the walls beyond me, I realized how silent my life usually is. Because my little bedroom is an addition, I rarely hear any noise within my walls. Arguments, singing and whining echoed beyond the door of the over-shared bathroom.

Scrubbing my dark hair into a lather, I sighed. I'd been

bathing under the pump in the front yard for far too long. The little bar of scented soap I found on a ledge shrank to a sliver as I lathered up my toes, knees, torso, arms, shoulders, and face. For the first time in ages, I felt truly clean.

Thoroughly drying my body and hair with a thin towel used up any energy I had left. Once again, I used the walls of the house to guide me back to my newly changed bed.

Sleep found me instantly. I dreamed of dead animals, endless babies, angry teachers.

Rapping at the door pulled me out of my much-needed slumber.

"Cat!" I croaked, "I can't, Cat, I'm sorry!"

The unlocked door popped open, and a figure leaned inside.

"It's me, Fleur." Hesitating only a moment, Peter walked in, shutting the door behind him. "Where's your lantern?"

"On the table. The matches are there too," I answered, rasping like a great-grandmother on her deathbed.

Soon a pleasant gleam presented me the ability to see my favorite human being, standing awkwardly with his straw hat in hand.

"Fleur, for God's sake! You look terrible!"

"You really know how to flatter a lady," I responded.

"My sisters heard you were dead. That's what everyone's saying at school."

"No one's killed me yet," I drawled.

"No," he agreed, "but they might try."

"This was natural. Pneumonia, I think," I assured him.

"Yes, Fleur, but they were all...happy when they thought you were...gone." His head hung toward the floor.

"I'll be careful, Peter." My breathing was still labored, but I no longer felt as though a jungle animal had taken up residence on my chest. Whatever medicine Father and John Junior had been plying me with had done its duty. "Peter, what's it like out there?" Curiosity gave me a quick burst of adrenaline.

"It's so strange. Men I've known my whole life act differently after we've crossed into the city. I've only been to the apartment once. There is a refrigerator full of things we've only read about; lunchmeat, soda, and leftover Chinese food. I played a round of Mortal Kombat. It's pretty violent, but I liked it."

"What about delivery? What's that like?" I was eager to hear anything I could about the new things he had seen.

"People out there are so nice, Fleur. They aren't evil, I don't think. They have families, jobs, homes, lives. Everyone smiles, a lot."

It sounded like heaven to me.

"Anyway," he continued, "my father hasn't laid a hand on me since I joined my brothers. It's like a vacation, of sorts. Double, though, because he doesn't hurt me, *and* I get to reap the benefits of being on delivery."

Peter looked healthier. Happier, too.

"You'd better go, Peter. Who knows what would happen if you were caught consorting with the Devil?"

"Fleur," Peter began, "I met her. Your cousin, Chrys."

Sparks of new strength fired throughout my wasted body.

"What?" I questioned. "How?"

"She was trying to find John Junior. She was worried about you because you hadn't sent a response in a while." He leaned toward me, landing on one knee. "She looks so much like you. You could be twins."

"I couldn't write because I was ill." I looked at my hands.

"Write when you can," he advised. "She cares about you."

Peter bowed deeper, his lips landing on my cheek.

"I love you," he said, "and I'm so thankful you're still alive."

Peeking out the door, he slipped out as if he'd never been there at all.

Touching my face where Peter's lips had landed, I wished I could live on The Outside. Maybe then I could be happy and free.

I needed to find a way to escape. Surely Chrys and her mother would let me visit until I formulated a plan for the rest of my life. A life filled with books. With freedom!

A fit of residual coughing reminded me that I would not be capable of walking down the street, let alone formulating a grand escape through the river and across the border to The Outside.

I would heal.

I would become well.

*And then I would plan.*

## 15

Two more days passed before I finally felt like myself. Almost. The wives took turns bringing food to the outside of my door, and I even received some company.

Wee Lilac zipped into my room, an impish dimple denting her left cheek.

"Heard you were feelin' better, Shar'n." Cat had arrived with her, draped around her shoulders.

"Much better. Thank you, Lilac."

She surveyed the room, taking in my broken desk and the gloves draped over the top of it where I'd left them to dry so many nights ago.

"Is it true, Shar'n?"

"Is what true?"

"You almost died?" Cat jumped from her shoulders to my lap.

"I believe so."

"We're not supposed to talk about it," Wee Lilac began cautiously, "but lots of kids wondered if you even *could* die. I mean, with the stuff you can do, you know? Your powers."

No one but Peter had ever spoken so openly about it with me before.

"Well," I thought for a bit, "I believe now, more than ever, that I *am* capable of dying. When I was at my sickest, I think I heard an angel speaking to me. I felt God there, too."

Wee Lilac nodded her head, her eyes wide.

"Father made me well," I said.

"Yes, the wives weren't very happy about all the time he spent out here with you. Mama told him he should just leave you, and let nature take its course. He raised his hand at her, but he didn't hit her."

"That's good, I guess." I was surprised that my father would raise his hand to a wife over me.

"I guess I better scoot. We're not allowed to be on this side of the house." Wee Lilac tried to gather Cat, but he decided to stay with me. Shrugging, she reached for the door.

Stepping out into the back yard, she turned and looked at me with intensity.

"That angel you heard? I'll bet it was your Mama."

# 16

My return to school felt awkward, but then again, most things feel awkward for me. My classmates now stared openly at me, not making an attempt to hide their ogling as I took my seat at the way back of the classroom.

Of course, no one welcomed me back.

I was still easily exhausted but managed to make it through the day. Upon my return home, I found that my chores had already been completed. It looked as though I would be allowed a little more time for a full recovery. I'm sure this was Father's doing, and I was also certain the wives weren't terribly happy about having to pick up my slack.

I knew that Chrys must have heard about my health. Even so, a response to her last letter was past due. I was down to my last sheet of paper. The ink in my inkwell was also running out. I could write in pencil, but enjoyed the process of dipping the pen, and how crisp the letters looked on the page.

Sighing, I turned to the back of the book, looking for some inspiration on how I could come up with words to explain the loss of her two contraptions.

It turned out that I didn't need it. The two pieces had been placed back into the book, unwrapped. Father knew I had these items, yet he chose to allow me to keep them. I feared I would live the rest of my days waiting for the other shoe to drop, waiting to be called out and beaten for my disregard of the rules. The sting of my last whipping was gone, but the pain was burned into my memory.

*Dear Chrys,*

*I have been unwell. Pneumonia has kept me in bed for weeks. It was awful.*

*The book of Numbers isn't really about numbers, in the way you are thinking. However, there is quite a bit of counting involved, as you will soon learn. Men are counted. The dead are also counted. So, you see, there are numbers involved within the story. It's not my favorite book, but it is necessary to read everything in order to understand how it all fits together.*

*I am still easily tired but hope to send a longer letter with your next lesson.*

*God bless,*
*Rose of Sharon*

As always, Chrys had scratched short notes along the

Bible's pages.

"Weird name," she had written, with a long, loopy arrow pointing to "Azazel."

"Poor little goats," was printed out by one of the paragraphs about sacrifice. Included was a little circle with a frowning face inside.

Smiling, I removed the flat library and the music player, replacing her letter with mine. Wrapping the book with the white cloth, which has steadily become dirtier, I tied it closed with the length of string and decided to deliver it right away.

Instead of breakfast being cooked, dinner preparations were underway this time at John Senior's house. As I walked up to the door, the wives and some of their children crowded the front window, staring as I approached. When I knocked, they all stepped into the shadows of the kitchen. No one answered.

"Coming, coming!" John Senior yelled from inside, finally stepping out onto the porch next to me. "Well, if it isn't the girl who almost perished!" he chuckled. Pulling a handkerchief from his back pocket, he managed to cover his mouth before the chuckle turned into a curdled cough. From behind the handkerchief he drawled, "Good to see ye looking so *alive.*"

The twinkle in his rheumy eyes was unnerving.

"Yes, it was a difficult time. I'm much better now."

"Yes, yes," he said, wiping his lips, "that I can plainly see."

"Is John Junior home from The Outside yet?" I asked.

"Not yet. I can make sure he gets that, though, if ye'd like." He nodded at the package. "Any time I can do a favor, I gladly do. Never know when ye might need one repaid."

He reached for the book, but his hand made a detour, gripping my elbow instead. I hastily stepped away.

"Th-Thank you," I stuttered, handing the book to the old man.

I quickly turned and walked away from him, breathing too fast and too shallow, which made the world swim. Still, I continued walking until I reached the safety of my room.

A bowl of stew sat cold on my table. Even if it had been hot, I wouldn't have been able to eat it. There was something so strange, so…wrong about John Senior. Being near him made my stomach hurt, caused immediate nausea. It wasn't just that he beat and starved (and most likely murdered) his own children and their mothers.

It was that he was *kind* to me.

## 17

I'd seen neither hide nor hair of Father since he saved my life. Mr. Adams was the one to inform me that the decision was still not made regarding whether I should return to the Harvest the following week. I thought about all those hours in the hot sun, and my shoulders drooped. I was happy to be well but would welcome one more week away from the fields.

By Thursday afternoon, anxiety began to creep up from the soles of my feet, filling my entire body. By the time we were sitting through the last few moments of our last lesson, Mr. Adams turned to the class, about to tell us to gather our things as he did at the end of every day, when a woman rushed through the door.

"Tulip! Freesia! You must come with me!" she wailed.

Mr. Adams blocked the exit, asking, "What is the meaning of this?'

"It's my son, my Young Luke! He was injured during a delivery–" Before she could finish, she burst into tears. Mr.

Adams draped a reassuring arm around her shoulder.

"What? What?" Jasmine cried.

Luke's sisters ran to their mother.

"Will he live, Mother?" Freesia asked.

"They don't know yet. He was hit by one of their cars. His legs..." Beneath my teacher's arm, she fell to the ground.

"No!" screamed Jasmine. She pushed Luke's sisters out of the way, streaking out of the building.

The two sisters helped their mother stand, and the three of them left the room as the end-of-the-day-bell rang.

"Before we leave," Mr. Adams said, "let us say a prayer for Young Luke."

Bowing our heads, we repeated the words to a prayer begging God to spare the young man.

"Amen."

The girls departed from the school a little slower than usual, Young Luke's accident weighing heavily on their minds.

I thought about the day I spied Jasmine and her beau kissing behind the cow barn. It was before I had experienced being kissed. Now that I knew what it felt like to be held in the arms of the boy you loved, I understood the pain that Jasmine must be suffering.

*It could have been Peter,* repeated over and over in my brain.

*It could have been Peter.*

By the looks of it, Jasmine wasn't going to be able to hide her relationship with the injured boy any longer. She was almost sixteen, but they never would have been able to marry. Her father would have found someone with an established home to take her. She would have been folded into a family of already existing wives and children.

I couldn't imagine what kind of punishment would follow for her once the nature of their affiliation was revealed. My punishment would be the same if anyone ever knew about the time I spent behind the barn with Peter.

On the way home, I passed Young Luke's house. The wagons and horses of the delivery team were all lined up on the dirt road by the lawn. So many people crowded the porch that they spilled out onto the pathway leading up to the front door. Peter was probably a part of that group. Wailing could be heard as I walked, taking it all in. I hoped that Mr. Adams's prayer helped.

All but one of Father's wives were with the crowd down the street, so it was just the children who ran inside when I arrived. Standing alone in the yard, I decided to take out the garbage. It had been weeks since I'd done any chores, and who knew how long everyone would sit vigil at the injured man's house.

By the time I returned from feeding the pigs, darkness was near. A plate of chicken waited for me in my room. *Will I never be allowed to eat outside on the porch again? At least there I could hear my family.* It probably suited my family to keep me out of sight altogether. My time visiting with pneumonia probably helped them realize how peaceful the evening meal could be without being able to see me, sitting apart from them, but still in plain view.

The chicken tasted like dust as I continually pictured Peter being hit by a car on The Outside. Finally pushing it away, I climbed under the covers on my bed, turning on Chrys's library apparatus.

Without realizing it, I floated into slumber.

I awoke in confusion; I was so deep into sleep that the sudden movement made my heart skip a beat, fluttering wildly in my breast.

An arm was wrapped around my neck, the owner of it pressed up against my back. Our shadow bounced along the walls; a strange dance by a strange, large beast.

"What–" I tried to choke out a question, but the grip was too tight.

Another arm swung in front of my face, presenting a long, sharp knife.

It twinkled in the lantern's glow.

"You listen to me," a voice whispered in my ear. "You're coming with me, and if you try to get away, I'll kill you with this."

The arm wrenched me out of the bed, forcing me out the door in my bare feet. Pebbles and twigs poked into my soles, but I barely noticed, focusing instead on the weapon held in front of me. It was a reminder of the warning I had just received.

The moon was completely covered with clouds, making the tops of the houses look eerily invisible, as if they had been erased by a lurking giant.

We approached the house that had been crowded by people only hours before. Before we reached the front door,

I was quickly spun around.

Jasmine stood before me, a crazed look about her. Her hair stood high in a tangle as if she'd spent time wrenching it through her fists. A rip split the neckline of her dress, and a dark splatter dusted her white apron which could have only been blood.

"You," she stated with frightening calm, "are going to bring him back."

Young Luke had gone to be with the Lord.

Flashing the knife at me, she gestured toward the house. Carefully, I entered the front living area. To the right, a body lay on the kitchen table, surrounded by all shapes and sizes of candles. Jasmine and I were the only breathing people in the room.

"Where is everyone?" I whispered.

"They've gone to sleep because he's...not here anymore. They've just *gone to sleep!*" Hysteria colored her words. "Something has to be done. You have to fix him, you demon. *Bring my Luke back to life.*"

"I-I don't know if I can, Jasmine."

"Of course, you can, you witch. You bring him back, or I'll kill you. I'll kill you so slow that it will hurt. *I'll make you bleed.*"

I didn't doubt it. She had already proven that she wasn't squeamish about killing animals. And after all, to her I was just an animal too.

Approaching the body, I could see that his legs were missing. His pants had been torn away, and ragged bones lay in twin puddles of viscous blood. It was thick and it pooled up and spilled onto the floor. Blankets and towels lined the area beneath, soaked in the vital fluid.

Young Luke's arms were crossed on his chest, his eyes closed. They hadn't even had the chance to undress him— to really try to save him—before he was taken.

"Jasmine," I whispered. Her wild eyes swung toward my face, breaking the hold they had had on the corpse. "Even if I can bring him back, his legs—"

"I don't care! I don't care! I don't care!" Her voice grew louder, more impassioned.

Grabbing my arm, she yanked me toward the makeshift operating table. She finally let go of me but held her weapon toward my face with two hands. Dancing from foot to foot, she nodded at her former lover.

"Take off the gloves," she commanded.

I pulled them away, looking for a surface to put them on that wasn't covered in blood.

"Give them to me." Jasmine grabbed them and threw them away from her, onto the floor.

How young he looked. If not for the weak beard on his chin, he would have seemed a sleeping child. I was filled with sadness at this loss of young life.

"Do it!" Jasmine growled.

Gingerly placing my palms on his wide chest, I waited for the buzzing sensation, not really expecting to feel anything.

"Oh!" I breathed. There was a fizzle in my fingertips. It was barely there, but it was something.

"Yes!" Jasmine urged, aiming the knife closer to my

nose.

Power crept to my first knuckle, then my second. A blurred message tried to reach my brain.

*I didn't see it. I stepped right in front—*

"He says he didn't see the car," I told Jasmine.

"No kidding! Of course, he didn't see the car. He wouldn't have done this on purpose, you idiot!"

The hum receded; the power gone. I pulled my hands away with a sigh.

"What are you doing?" Jasmine shrieked. "You can't leave him like that! Bring him back! Bring him back!"

"I can't do it, Jasmine! He's been gone too long. I tried; I really did!"

The dead man's family was awake now.

Two children entered the room, then backed out, alarmed. Luke's father rushed toward us.

"What is going on here?"

"*What is going on here?*" Jasmine repeated. "I'll *tell you* what is going on here. I am going to kill this worthless, filthy abomination!" Her voice was so loud that neighbors began to arrive, trying to get a glimpse of the late-night drama.

Jasmine grabbed my hair in her fist, forcing me to kneel before her.

"What good is she if she can't bring my Luke back?" She sobbed. "She deserves to die, and go to hell, where she belongs!"

"Put the knife down, Jasmine!" a deep male voice commanded.

"No." She pulled my head back and rested the tip of her weapon against my tender skin, pausing.

The pause was just long enough for a rock to come flying from the front door, hitting my attacker in the head. The sharp edge of her knife grazed my throat, then it clattered to the kitchen floor. Jasmine collapsed behind me, unconscious.

Pandemonium ensued. Two men rushed inside to collect Jasmine, holding her arms behind her back. I put my hand up to my wound, feeling the wet trickle through my fingers. I made the mistake of pulling my hand away for a look.

Funny how I had no qualms about touching dead things, but faced with my own blood, I couldn't seem to hang on to consciousness.

# 18

My hands searched the surface I was lying on before I opened my eyes. My bare fingers recognized my blankets.

*It had only been a dream! A terrible dream!*

I found Father sitting at the foot of my bed. A wide bandage was wrapped around my neck. It had not been a dream, after all.

Father cleared his throat. "Rose of Sharon," he gently said, "I have something that needs to be said."

Sitting up, I pulled my legs up toward my chest, afraid of what he would tell me.

"My wives can't have you here any longer. They are afraid for their children. Our children." For once he met my gaze with his eyes. They were troubled.

"But where will I go, Father? No one will have me." Even though I spent a fair amount of time fantasizing about escaping to The Outside, I had nothing, no money, no skills. How would I even get there?

"That is not entirely true." He seemed awfully uncomfortable. Taking a deep breath, he explained, "John Senior says he will have you."

My face flushed with panic. *John Senior?*

"He has offered to marry you. You are to go to his home immediately."

"But Father," I reasoned, "custom dictates that we must be engaged at least two weeks."

"Sometimes following customs isn't possible. You will be in his home, which is indecent if you've not married. He has promised to keep you separated from the rest of the household for two days. Then an Elder will visit the house to perform the ceremony."

"But Father–" I sobbed.

He shook his head, holding up a hand to quiet me.

"Pack your things. I will escort you to his house. You have ten minutes to prepare yourself."

My father handed me my gloves, and then stepped outside, leaving me to absorb the terrible news that he'd just given me.

I would be one of John Senior's wives in two days' time.

The short walk was covered in silence. Father carried my pitifully small bag, filled with my change of clothes wrapped around Chrys's gifts. They were really my only belongings. I left my near-empty inkwell on my desk, as well as the dry pen. I hoped Wee Lilac might find them, thinking of me whenever they were used.

We reached the wraparound porch a lot sooner than I

would have liked.

John Senior sat on the top step, twirling his mustache. Waiting for me.

"Well, girl, look at that! Another favor, eh. Looks like I've got a couple of them in the bank now."

"Father," I begged, hoping he might change his mind.

*Maybe he could finally tell his wives that I am his daughter, that I am a part of the family, too.* I thought.

"She knows about the time. Two days. You promised." Father stared at his dusty boots as he talked.

"Yes, yes, sure. Two days. I got a room all ready for her. No one'll bother her." He took my bag from Father's grip with gnarled, thickly veined hands.

"Travel light, eh?" he smirked.

"Goodbye, Rose of Sharon," Father nearly whispered, his face ashen.

"Father, please look after Cat for me. Give him to Wee Lilac. She likes him."

He didn't answer, just walked away with his fists buried in his pockets.

## 19

J ohn Senior brought me to a small office, passing by many of his wives and children, who all stared open-mouthed as I walked down the hall. A tall shelf covered one wall, full of books. A leather-covered chair was pushed into a highly polished wooden desk, stacked high with papers. Another wall was covered by a long, fabric upholstered couch with a stack of blankets sitting on one arm.

"This is where ye'll stay for the next two days," John Senior explained, eyeing me up and down as he closed the office door. "Please sit down. Make yerself comfortable."

*As though that could be possible.*

Gingerly, I took a seat on the couch.

"Now I know I don't have to tell ye not to touch m'books. Don't touch nothin' on the desk, neither. Ye hear?"

I nodded my head.

"Do you want to know why I want ye so bad, when no

one else can stand to look at ye?" Sitting on the edge of his desk, he leaned toward me with glee in his eye.

*I don't care,* I wanted to scream.

"I've got a coughing sickness. Had it for years, but it's gettin' real bad." As if to demonstrate, he pulled out his handkerchief, hacking and spitting into it. After studying it and wadding it up, he stuffed it back into his pocket.

"Now," he began again, "Seeing how I keep saving yer sorry butt, it looks like ye really do owe me a pretty good favor. I don't want any kids from ye, 'cause we don't need any more like ye out there scaring The People. No one'll eat any food ye cook, neither. I hear ye got some laundry skills, but I got a lot of women and girls—plenty to cover that chore."

John Senior opened an elaborately carved wooden box on his desk, choosing a fragrant cigar. He rolled it under his nose for a while, enjoying the smell of it. Then he lit it, taking a healthy puff before he began to speak again.

"To pay me back for my kindnesses to ye, all I want ye to do is bide time till I up and die. Stay near to me every day, right by my side, at all times. When I die, ye'll be there, waiting to bring me back." He laughed heartily, as if it was all a big joke.

But he was completely serious.

"I'm not afraid of them things," he said, gesturing to my hands. "In fact, give 'em here."

I stood and approached the desk. He pulled my gloves off, stopped for a moment to gather courage, then used my wrists to flip them over, palms up.

His wrinkled, scarred hands hovered above mine, his eyes burning. Wheezing, he lowered them, connecting our skin. After holding them like that for a few seconds, breathing hard, he pulled away.

"I always told people there's nothin' to worry about. Ye're the girl that brings things back, not takes things away."

Sitting in his big leather chair, John Senior smoked his cigar, focusing on my face. It made me feel naked, as though he was reading my thoughts, looking inside of me.

"I was there, ye know, on that day. My God." He whistled. "How that field looked, all them flowers popping upright. I never seen the colors look that vivid before, neither. And the look on them boys's faces." His laugh ended in a fit of phlegm-filled coughing. "Now look where we are—I got myself a necromancer for a wife!"

When nothing but a nub remained between his fingers, he smashed the cigar into a glass ashtray and stood.

"I got to lock ye up. Ye understand, right? Don't want no one gettin' any funny ideas. Not you. Not them out there, neither. I'll bring ye yer meals." And he left.

I heard the scrape of the key locking me inside.

# THE OTHER PEOPLE

# CHRYS

M om was still pissed at me for connecting with Rose
of Sharon. The only words she'd said were
"Splenda," when she wanted me to pass her the sweetener
for her coffee and I was leaning up against the cabinet that
had it inside, and "Working tonight." She pretended like I
wasn't there, passing next to me without a glance.

It started to wig me out.

Grammy Esther said she was just worried and it would
all eventually work its way out. The thing is, I didn't think I
could work it out without telling my cousin that I couldn't
write to her anymore. What my mom didn't know (and
couldn't know, or she'd stop me for sure) was that I was
building the damn friendship to help her.

When we figured out that Rose of Sharon liked to read,
I sent her my Kindle. I got an iPad Mini for my birthday
('cause I liked Grammy Esther's so much) and that's how I
read all my eBooks now. I knew that girl would get a kick
out of all the books I had in the Kindle, because most of it

was teeny-bopper stuff. I doubted she had access to anything like that in The Wacko's Land. She'd obviously read most of the classics. Grammy realized, days later, that the quote she couldn't identify in the last letter was from *The Outsiders*, by S.E. Hinton. I hadn't read it, but the boys on the cover from the movie were H.O.T. I still didn't really want to read the book, but I decided I might take a peek and see if I could find it on Netflix.

The way Mom acted when that guy dropped off the Bible was seriously weird. She was one of the most self-assured people that I'd ever met. If you looked under the word "confidence" in the dictionary Mom's picture would have probably been there. When that man came over, though, she was all flustered. She seemed almost *shy*.

When I wanted to send that bulky old Bible to my cousin, with a new and improved shipping container carved into the back of it, I headed to the streets to find the handsome guy with the reddish beard who made my mother behave like a timid little girl. For a minute or two I realized how crazy my plan was. I mean, we lived in a smallish town, but it was still *a town*. And there were a LOT of those old-fashioned wagon/buggy thingies around all the time. But I found him. Actually, he saw me first. Almost ready to give up, I sat outside at Starbucks. I didn't buy anything, just needed a break after all that walking around, being all Sherlock Holmes and stuff.

He sat down across from me, saying, "I presume that is for me. Or rather, for Rose of Sharon?" His eyes were all twinkly, and he had a great smile. I almost got why Mom

174

acted so funny when she saw him.

"Yeah," I said. "Can you make sure she gets it?" I pushed the cloth-covered bundle across the wrought iron table.

"Of course." Tipping his hat, he carried the Bible away, loading it onto one of the buggies.

The letter I got back was too funny. That girl was pretty good at writing in code. I totally understood that the battery had died, and that she was enjoying reading the *Twilight* series. I hadn't bothered sending a charger because Mom had told me that they didn't use electricity. They had indoor plumbing, which is against the popular belief of anyone who gets all obsessed with The People—but no electricity.

If I ever got to meet Rose of Sharon in person, I would confess I never really read that Bible. Whenever she sent an assignment, I popped on over to my iPad and made a quick visit to Wikipedia. I chose a couple of interesting points and added 'em into my letter, sure to pencil in a few comments in the actual book, so we would still have an excuse to send the big thing back and forth.

The next delivery included my old iPod. Now that I had an iPhone, I didn't really use it anymore. I remembered Mom talking about how music is forbidden where my cousin lives, and that they are allowed to sing in church and in the fields, but that *is it*. And when they're picking those flowers, they sing the same stuff from church.

I thought Rose of Sharon might appreciate a little Coldplay. I also included U2 and just enough Red Hot Chili

Peppers to get her hooked.

When she returned the Kindle and the iPod to be recharged, I knew my plan had worked!

How could she *not* want to come live with us after seeing all the cool stuff we had?

# JOHN JUNIOR

I was in love with Iris the moment I saw her. I had been in love with her for so long that I didn't remember what it felt like to not be in love with her. When I first discovered I couldn't live without her, she was called Catherine.

She tracked her sister to The People's Land. It could've been anywhere to her, which really bothered the Elders, who all have great pride in their community. After a while, she fit in pretty well, and most people didn't even remember that she came from The Outside—or at least they no longer minded.

When she first arrived, she didn't have a clue where she would live. She stayed with Dark Joseph and Lily for a spell, but the Elders think it indecent for an unwed woman to sleep in a man's house if he isn't her husband.

Joseph and Lily's situation was unique. They met while Joseph was making flower deliveries. She was a waitress at a coffee shop we all frequented, while on The

Outside. Although I found her attractive and charming, I didn't understand the intensity with which Joseph worshipped her. A few fathers had already approached my friend, offering the hands of their daughters, but Joseph hadn't accepted an offer yet. It was as though he knew she was out there, waiting for him.

Custom dictated that a man and woman should be engaged for at least two weeks before the marriage ceremony was completed. Lily and Joseph became engaged almost immediately, once he explained the terms. She continued to live with her sister, in the apartment they shared. When the fourteen days were up, she made the short trip through the flat land and stones by taxi, carrying only one suitcase. Joseph was waiting at the bridge, key in hand. I came with him, and when I glimpsed Catherine in the car, looking glum, I approached the open window.

I knew about Lily's sister. She was a beloved topic of conversation for Lily. What I didn't know, was that meeting her would make me feel like I had finally discovered the meaning of life. My senses seemed to immediately sharpen, everything becoming clearer: the outlines around the rocks, the smell of dust, the sound of the idling taxi.

"Hello, Catherine." I felt shy, like a teenage boy.

"Hi." Her eyes were clear blue pools of sadness.

"She'll be happy, Catherine. I'm sure of it." I looked behind me to see the betrothed pair engaged in a very long kiss.

"I know. It's just..." She shook her head, looking

down.

"You're all alone now," I finished for her. I had never wanted to console anyone before. Living in my father's house, with all that happens on a daily basis, I suppose I had become a bit hardened. Desensitized. All that went away as I stood helpless, watching Catherine's face crumble.

"I'll be okay," she whispered. To my ears it sounded much more like a question than a statement.

"You will." Surprised, I noted this sounded like a question as well.

The lovely, sad girl in front of me sniffled, shrugging.

"I'm John," I said, lamely.

"Hello, John."

Lily approached the car, hands linked with Joseph, and leaned toward her sister.

"Please watch out for Grammy Esther and let her look after you."

Catherine reached through the window, and Lily grasped it, tightly.

"I love you, Emily," Catherine said.

"You know I had to change my—" Lily began.

"I know. I just had to say it, one more time." Catherine sat back in her seat, releasing her sister's hand.

She tapped on the glass between herself and the driver, letting him know that she was ready to leave.

The cab kicked up a cloud of dust, traveling slowly along the bumpy dirt road. Lily hesitated for a moment, then linked arms with Joseph and gestured toward the gate;

toward the marriage ceremony waiting on the other side.

Their feet made hollow noises along the bridge as they crossed. The sound wasn't half as hollow as my heart felt, watching the car as it carried Catherine away.

# CHRYS

Holy crap, my mom looked awful. She was cold all the time and wore a sweater constantly, even though we were almost to summer, and it was pretty much always super-hot out. She was the size of an elementary school student and had this awful cough. She'd even started bringing a handkerchief with her everywhere, like all old-timey, and stuff. She would say a couple of words, and then start coughing into the little fabric square. If someone made her laugh, it was a guaranteed cough-starter.

Things went sour with Brendan and I couldn't even talk to her about it, and she was the best advice-giver on the planet. *My friends* even asked her for boy advice! Brendan wanted to do more than just kissing, but I wasn't ready for it so he dumped me. Lauren acted like she was sympathetic, but the gleam in her eye told me that she was glad what she had with Steven had outlasted my sad little excuse for a romance.

At least I got to have a romance, I suppose. Mom told

me that you get married at sixteen when you live in The People's Land. Like, you get pulled right out of school and everything. And you didn't get to pick your husband; your dad got to pick.

Since Mom didn't grow up there, she did get to choose. She chased after her sister but needed to figure out a way to stick around. Some old guy said he'd marry her, and she jumped at the chance. She loved my aunt so much that she would have done anything to stay. She was only eighteen then. Both girls moved out of their parents' house so young! *Ran away* would be a more truthful way to put it, since they were both teenagers, had almost no money and just wanted to get out fast. The irony was that my grandparents were, like, super religious, and wouldn't let their daughters go to rock concerts, date, or stay out late at night. Not to mention my step-grandmother trying to kill them, and stuff. The girls ran away for freedom and became prisoners in the process. My mom was a prisoner, anyway. From what she's let slip, my aunt was happy where she was. Then again, *she* got to pick her man. But then she died, and there wasn't anything left to hold Mom in her jail. They tried, but they failed.

Meanwhile, she had to pick flowers all the time and got skin cancer as a result. And then the cancer spread to other places. She'd gotten sicker than ever but wouldn't say anything about it to her own daughter.

I wanted to talk to her about what was happening, but since she was still not talking to me *at all* made that idea impossible. So, I decided I'd go around acting like everything was A-OK, even though it was starting to make me nuts.

Grammy Esther still talked to me. She tried to explain what my mother was probably feeling. I understood that she never wanted to return to the place where I was born, I really did. I also understood that the husband she'd left was so awful that she wouldn't ever speak about him. She let it slip once that the man she was forced to marry beat his wives (as in, Mom wasn't the only wife) and kids and that he was a mean old man, and leaving him was the second-best thing she'd ever done.

The best was having me.

# JOHN JUNIOR

J oseph and Lily were married in a simple ceremony, as
all marriages in The People's Land were. I'd delivered
dozens of flowers to hundreds of weddings, and I learned
that people on The Outside love their weddings. Live
music! Special, formal clothing! Ice sculptures, white table
clothes, and hundreds of the Opus Dei! It was nothing like
the way we celebrated the joining of two hearts.

Only immediate family, the bride, the groom, and a
Host Elder were involved. Joseph's father had passed away
years before, so it was just his mother there with them
inside the house Joseph built for his new wife. The
ceremony took less than a half hour, beginning with the
Host Elder's reminders of what makes a good wife and
good husband. He then recited quotes from the Bible
dealing with marriage and the love between a man and
woman. Both made promises to remain true to each other
and to God.

I'd seen this all many times because my father had

many wives.

I waited on the porch for my friends to exit, along with some others from the community, all of us well-wishers straining to hear the ceremony inside.

When Joseph and Lily stepped through the door, love and happiness surrounded them like a giant halo. Joseph's mother followed behind, looking a bit annoyed. I hugged my friend, kissing his new bride on the cheek. Smiles and handshakes were generously distributed.

That was the first day of the rest of their lives.

I went home to my father's house. All the women and children looked as miserable as ever going through the motions of what made a life under John Senior's rule.

I couldn't stop thinking about Catherine.

Days passed, and my need to find her, to make sure she was all right, filled my every thought. Whenever I saw Lily, her resemblance to Catherine made me stutter, bumbling around like a lunatic.

I had to see her.

# CHRYS

I got a new letter from my cousin, charged both the Kindle and the iPod, wrote another fake note about how into this religion stuff I was, and then decided to send them back as soon as I could find someone in one of the black buggies to take them. A couple of days later, I found that guy waiting at our front door. He was sitting on the floor, his back against the wall, straw hat hanging from his hands.

"I was in town, and thought I'd see if you needed me."

"Oh, I...uh."

"I'm sorry if I frightened you. I just know that there has been a correspondence going on and I–" He stood awkwardly, looking way uncomfortable.

"Oh, no—really! It's okay." I fumbled with my key, opening the door, "Please, come on in."

He hovered near the entrance—which I left open so Grammy would hear me if I had to scream or anything— while I went down the hall to my room to pick up the package.

"Just wait right there," I called to him.

When I got back to the entryway, I found him looking at all the pictures hung along the walls and covering pretty much every surface in the whole apartment.

"These are so nice," he commented, moving along to the next one.

"Yeah, my mom is, like, obsessed with pictures."

"It's a good way to record history, isn't it?" He lingered on a photo of my mother all dressed up for my middle school graduation, looking like a knockout in her strapless black minidress.

"I guess so." It was sort of starting to creep me out, how intense he was looking at the pictures and everything. So, I said, "Uh, here's the mail."

"Oh, of course," he said, taking the package from me. "Thank you."

"Any time," he promised. "I'll check in again, soon. But if you need me, you know where to look. Just find an old-fashioned horse and cart, and whoever's driving will know where I am. I'm the only one that makes these deliveries for Shar'n."

"Thank you," I said, walking toward the front door, trying to *hint-hint* tell him it was time to go.

"Goodbye, Chrysanthemum," he smiled.

*Hearing him say my full name didn't even feel all that weird.*

# JOHN JUNIOR

E ven while preparing and loading the wagons for delivery there was a spring in my step. Flower delivery wasn't the most important thing that was going to happen on The Outside that day.

I was going to pay a surprise visit to Catherine.

When we reached the bridge, I took out the key and unlocked the double lock, opening the gate wide. It was how every delivery began; the wagons lined up to cross.

I signaled for the first buggy to move through the wooden frame of the gate. The horse clip-clopped across the wooden surface, followed by the next three freights. When the last had crossed, they all waited in a line for me to lock the door and hop onto the last wagon.

But she was there, waiting.

"I'm sorry, John, I–" Her eyes were red, and she looked so, so tired. A navy-blue duffle bag sat at her feet.

"Have you been waiting here all night?" I asked in alarm. I noticed that her shirt was made of thin material, and she shivered, arms wrapped around her torso.

Nodding her head, she looked away.

"Head out!" I called to the caravan waiting to depart. The curious eyes of all the men on the delivery crew followed our conversation, crowding the windows for a view of the scene.

Taking off my coat, I draped it over her shoulders. She looked up at me, gratefully. Those eyes made my insides swim. I wanted badly to touch her.

"I couldn't stay out here without her," Catherine mumbled.

*I couldn't stay in here without you,* I thought.

Walking the short distance to her sister's house without exchanging any words, we arrived to find Lily in the garden that Joseph had begun for her in anticipation of her arrival. He was already down at the blue building, working with his numbers.

Lily didn't see us until we were almost upon her. When she finally noticed our arrival, she squealed in joy and squeezed her sister in a hearty hug, lifting her feet right up off the ground.

"Somehow I knew you would come," Lily said through happy tears.

# CHRYS

When my mom came home last night, I heard her bustling in the kitchen. I could tell that she'd pulled a frozen dinner out of the freezer, and I even heard the microwave beep. Then nothing. The microwave beeped again, saying, "Hey! I already told you I was done!" It beeped two more times, and then I knew for sure that something was wrong.

I found her on the kitchen floor, half leaning against the bottom row of cupboards, legs at a funny angle.

"Mom!" I shook her, alarmed. "Mom! Are you all right?"

She moaned, opening her eyes.

"God, Chrys, I'm sorry." It was the longest sentence she'd spoken to me in, like, forever.

I got her a glass of water, and she seemed to wake up a little more.

"Do we need to go to the hospital?"

"No!" she insisted, sitting up straighter, blinking her

eyes.

"Do I need to get Grammy?" I had already started toward the front door.

"No, Chrys, no. I'm fine."

"You don't look so 'fine,' Mom."

"I'll be alright. Just let me drink this water, okay? I think I might be a little dehydrated." She sipped at the glass, finally standing up, but using the counter to lean on.

"So, like, are we gonna talk about how sick you are, or what?" Sometimes my mouth ran away before I could catch it. Mom always said it was my worst quality.

No comment.

"Hey, Mom, do you think maybe we should see a doctor if you're going to be passing out on the kitchen floor? Cause, like, if you're planning to make a regular routine of it and everything, then–"

"Will you just shut up, Chrys?" She shook her head in annoyed amazement.

"Well, fill me in, please. I mean, jeez, Mom! It's not like I'm stupid, you know. I can totally tell how sick you're getting!"

"Oh, Chryssy, I'm so sorry." Moving to the dining table, she sat down. Resting her chin on her folded hands, she smiled a sad little smile. "Yes, the cancer is back. Yes, it's very bad."

Even though I already basically knew, hearing her say it made it way more real.

"What are we going to do?" I asked, already tearing up a bit.

"Nothing, Honey. We are going to do nothing."

"What do you mean? There're drugs! Chemo, and stuff!" I sat across from her.

"I don't want to do that, Chrys." She reached across the table, holding my hand. "It's spread to…well, to a lot of places. I would be in the hospital, constantly. Even then, I wouldn't have all that long to…" She squeezed my hand. "I want to continue like everything's fine, okay? Total denial—that's what I choose. Instead of being sick all the time, away from you and Grammy and my comfortable bed—and then dropping dead suddenly *anyway*, I choose life. God is the only one who knows when I'm scheduled for a departure. I'd rather go along as usual, doing what I love with the *people* I love until it's no longer an option. I mean, people fall off cliffs or crash in airplanes and die all the time, right? They don't get to choose some sort of preventative medication to keep them going miserably along?"

"You believe in God? After all the pain He's caused you, Mom? Really? After what you went through with your parents, with your sister? How can you believe in Him after all that?" The tears were now falling freely, dropping in a wet splatter on the table.

"Of course I believe in God, Honey. You must believe in Him, too. Bad things have happened, but the good have always outweighed the bad. For example, if I hadn't run away from home, I never would have found this apartment or met Esther. If I hadn't followed your aunt to The People's Land, I wouldn't have had you. And if I hadn't needed to escape, we wouldn't have come back here to Grammy Esther, and our very wonderful, very comfortable life. He has a plan, Chrys; He always has a plan…It's just…hard to know what it is, sometimes."

"Well, this part of His plan really sucks."

# JOHN JUNIOR

C atherine stayed that first night with Joseph and Lily, and no one bothered them. I couldn't stay away, stopping by just to catch a glimpse of her face. It was now as familiar to me as the Opus Dei and no less beautiful.

We talked through the evening, the girls recounting stories of their childhood, laughing at many of the memories. We compared life on The Outside to The People's Land, not really all that surprised by the feeling that we and they were from completely different planets. Lily served coffee cake and we ate in companionable silence.

"I could live here," Catherine announced. "It's so different, but if you're here, I'll manage. No matter what." She looked at her sister fondly.

I bid them all good night, walking home on cloud feet to the house with the wraparound porch. I didn't even realize when I reached the front door. Father sat on the top step, smoking a heavily scented cigar.

"Where ye been, boy?" he asked, warily. "I hear ye deserted the delivery team this mornin'."

"Father, I didn't exactly desert them. They've done it hundreds of times, and nothing went wrong. I made sure to request a full report when they returned."

"Ye was with that girl, weren't ye? The Outsider's sister?" My father smirked.

An icy warning crawled from my scalp to my shoulders. I didn't know how to interpret it.

My face must have given me away.

"Thought so," he laughed. "Ye best be stayin' away from them girls. They don't know how things're s'posed to be 'round here, just yet. They need to be broken in, see? They need to be trained." His sunken eyes gleamed.

"Good night, Father," I said, disgusted. I entered the house to find my room in the back of the building.

My father truly hated women. There wasn't a reason for the boiling animosity, as far as I could tell. Some people just have something in them that feeds on malice, I've learned. My father was one of them. His loathing and contempt toward the female of our species was legendary within our community.

Unfortunately for the wives and children with whom I shared a house, I was the only male child he had ever created.

\*\*\*

The next morning, the Elders came to visit the

newlyweds before Joseph had gone. This living arrangement was indecent, they warned. They had two choices: Either Catherine returned to The Outside, or she accepted a husband.

I didn't learn about the ultimatum until the next day.

Things might have been so much different if I had heard about it sooner.

# CHRYS

L ike usual, I couldn't keep a damn secret to save my life. Luckily, Grammy Esther was a pro at keeping things to herself, so she was a great receptacle for all the problems I always seemed to have, some more serious than others.

"Yes, I know." Grammy said, when I told her about Mom's health.

"You know?"

"Yes, she told me."

She told Grammy Esther and not me? What was this, the *keep-important-things-from-Chrysanthemum-Perkins game?*

"Don't be angry," Grammy said, "she knew you wouldn't handle this part very well…"

"Handle *what* part well? My mom choosing to die, instead of trying to get help? *You mean that part?*" Sarcasm had always been my best defense mechanism against pretty much every emotion you can name. Fear, sorrow, anger, hurt; if you threw some feels in my direction, I'd find the words to cleverly bite your head off.

This time it sounded bitter and ugly, and I wished desperately that I could take it all back.

Plopping onto the doily-laden couch, I wrapped my forehead in my hands.

"Well, it looks like I'm going to have to get my cousin here sooner than I thought."

"What do you mean, *yakira*?" Grammy asked, sitting down next to me.

"She's got powers, Grammy. She brings dead stuff back to life. If she's here when Mom dies..." I didn't finish, expecting her to connect her own dots.

"Chrys, it is impossible, what you are saying. There is no power like the one you speak of!"

"Yeah, there is, and Rose of Sharon has it. I heard all about it from Mom herself."

"Impossible." Grammy looked at me closer, as if to see whether I was making a funny.

"Yeah, it's impossible." I looked just as closely back at her. "But it's true."

# JOHN JUNIOR

I returned from a day of deliveries, eager to see Catherine. I saw her all day long in every beautiful thing I encountered. The flowers reminded me of her lovely smile, and the sky couldn't compete with the blue of her eyes.

I was definitely in big trouble.

Whistling my way up the path to Joseph's front door, my pulse quickened at the thought of seeing her. *I will tell her tonight*, I decided, *that I am in love with her.* Holding it inside was making me physically ill. The only cure would be a full confession.

Lily answered when I rapped my knuckles on the door. Her solemn face should have bespoken the drama about to unfold, but I was still flying high with the anticipation of professing my love to her sister. My Catherine.

Joseph sat on one side of the couch, his dark hairy chin pinched between a thumb and forefinger, elbow resting on the arm of his seat. Catherine sat on the other side, face paler than china, eyes glassy and unfocused.

I fell to the ground at Catherine's feet.

"What is it? What has happened?" Panic soaked my words.

"She's to be married," Lily answered behind me.

Catherine's head dipped, a sob escaping her chest.

"Who? Who is it?" Snapping to attention, I rose to my feet, ready to go to battle.

"It's the only way I could stay, John," Catherine muttered.

"Who?" I asked through clenched teeth.

No one was willing to answer me.

"Who?" I groaned.

"Your father," Joseph whispered.

# CHRYS

Mom let information about Rose of Sharon slip on two occasions. Both times she was drinking too much wine. Both times she told me all kinds of things about her life before we became Escapees, like about how her husband liked to whip his wives with his belt. A belt with an obnoxiously large metal buckle. And when I say "liked", I mean *liked*. Some people liked watching movies, some liked to train for marathons, some liked to shop. My father liked to beat the women who lived under his roof. He also liked to starve and humiliate them. He was a bit gentler with the children, of which there were many, but *a bit gentler* is a relative term when dealing with a sadist.

The first time Mom spoke of Rose of Sharon, I was intrigued. I had relatives out there, somewhere, and one of them was a girl my age. I wanted to hear everything that I could. She looked like me, I learned. We created our own language when we were little and would speak all day without my mother ever knowing what we were saying.

The one thing that was different between the two of us was that she could raise the dead. *No biggie.*

Mom didn't even realize that she knew what she knew at first. One time she found Rose of Sharon at the outside water pump, crying. When she asked what was wrong, the child said that she needed soap. *The rat told her that he had been poisoned, so she should wash her hands after touching him,* she explained. "I don't want to have to go asleep forever," the little girl sobbed.

The next time Mom saw something weird, there was no doubt about what she knew. She saw Rose of Sharon approach a baby bird who had fallen out of its nest. There were other babies still in the tree, but this one had somehow tumbled loose. It shuddered and fell still.

"It's okay, birdie," the two-year-old crooned. "I fix you; I make you better."

Holding the bird in a pod made of her two little hands, the little niece held her ear against them, nodding.

"I know," the child said, "I miss my mommy, too."

When her hands opened, the bird, who had clearly breathed its last breath mere minutes before, hopped onto the grass. Not much later, the mother bird swooped down to recapture her offspring.

"She fell. She wanted her Mama," the child explained when she saw that her Aunt Iris had witnessed the event.

My mother told her that she mustn't ever do things like that again. The little girl agreed, but Mom occasionally still saw Rose of Sharon whisper into her cupped palms, listening for a response.

But only when she thought no one was watching.

# JOHN JUNIOR

A thirst for blood like I had never before known filled my senses, scaring the other three people in the room.

"I'll kill him," I growled.

As I started toward the door with murder in my heart, Joseph grabbed both of my arms, pulling me to the ground on my stomach. He pinned me down with his knee on my back and held me still. The only sound that filled the room was my rattling breath.

"It was the only way," Catherine said, the life flown out of her.

"It couldn't have been the only way, Catherine. I would have done it. I would have married you!" Not exactly the romantic declaration I had planned.

"Oh, John." She slid to the floor next to me, and Joseph eased up a bit, letting me turn to hear what she had to say. "They suggested that. Lily and Joseph did. We tried, but–"

"But what? I want to hear everything." Joseph finally released his hold and stepped away, and I leaned against the couch.

"It was the Elders," Lily began, "they said you were too young yet. They said that they already had someone willing to marry her. Someone who had an established household. They made her sign a contract, telling her that if she didn't do it, they'd throw her out. We were terrified."

"I was at work," Joseph announced, miserably.

"I didn't even know who it was until after," Catherine explained.

"You don't understand," I lamented. "My father isn't worthy of you. He's filled with– with evil. He'll hurt you, Catherine!"

"He has other wives," she said, quietly determined. "Surely there's safety in numbers. I'll be all right. And I'll be able to stay."

And that was when my fate was sealed. I thought I loved her before.

Now I loved her more than ever for her bravery.

# CHRYS

G rammy still didn't quite believe me, but since she loved my mom like a daughter, she was up to trying anything that might help.

"When did you last hear from this girl?" Grammy asked, a few days after I confided in her about my crazy plan. Code name: Seduce the Small-Town Girl With Big-Town Electronics. Not really, but that was pretty much the gist of it.

"That's the thing." I chewed my thumbnail. "Usually, she's pretty good about being regular with her writing and everything. Especially now that she needs to send the Kindle and iPod back to be charged. I haven't heard from her in weeks, though, and I'm a little bit worried."

"Why not just tell her what you need her for, Chrys? Why all the secret shenanigans? Why be a *meshuga*? Just *tell her* you want her powers to save your mother! This is her aunt, after all. How could she say no?" It sounded logical, but there was this weird little thumbtack of doubt wedged in my brain. It just wouldn't allow for removal; it was stuck in really good, like when I wanted to make sure that the posters in my room wouldn't fall down. Ever.

"I dunno. I've come this far with the plan, so I kinda want to follow through. Know what I mean?"

"Yes. I know what you mean." Grammy laid a reassuring hand on my shoulder.

After I left her apartment, I headed for downtown. About twelve blocks from where I live, two of the creepy old, black buggies were parked at the curb. A man sat in the driver's seat in each one. One of the men was gigantic and had a thick beard, which kind of intimidated me. The other one was sort of skinny, and he was wearing a hat, but his hair managed to still look messy, curling around the edges of the brim. I chose that one.

"Uh, excuse me?" I called, which made him jump a little in his seat.

"Hello," he answered in a soft voice. He had kind eyes and freckles dusting his nose.

"I'm looking for...well, darn. I don't actually know who I'm looking for. I don't know his name. I've been sending letters to my cousin, Rose of Sharon. She lives where you do, I think." *Because, hey, there could totally be another group of Amish-looking people delivering flowers in town, right now.*

"Yes!" He had a spectacular smile. "You're looking for John Junior. He'll make your delivery for you." He winked at me.

"That's sort of the problem. I've been waiting for my

cousin to answer my last letter, and, well, she's usually so good about responding, but it's been a long time since I last heard from her. I have to admit, I'm a little bit worried."

Kindness filled the boy's eyes. He was actually sort of handsome. If you took away the stupid hat and gave him some cargo shorts, who knew?

"Listen," he said, "I know her—your cousin. I'll tell her you're waiting for a letter. If she knows you're worried about her, she'll send one right way. I'm sure of it. Rose of Sharon is … she's a very special girl." I could tell that he struggled to find a description for her.

"Okay." I thanked him and walked away, taking one more look over my shoulder before I turned the corner.

The boy was staring at his hands, looking extremely concerned.

# JOHN JUNIOR

Returning home to seek out my father, my head was filled with violent scenarios. They all involved patricide, and different ways I could kill *him*; slowly or quickly, with lots of blood or none at all. My hands shook, and my ears hurt from clenching my jaw.

Waiting on the porch, he sat with another cigar puffing blue smoke into the darkening sky.

"Why?" I choked.

"Oh, come now, boy. Are those tears I see comin'? Are ye some sort of sissy, now? Over a damn woman?" Oh, how he taunted me.

"But you knew. You knew how I felt! Of all the women in The People's Land, why did you have to take this one?"

"Well, it seems like you owe me, son. Ye took yer mama from me when you were born. No matter what, I'm still down a wife. The way I sees it, this is just ye repaying your debt to me." Taking a long puff, he had the audacity to smile.

A vision filled my head of my fist knocking out whatever yellowed teeth he had remaining.

Instead, I wiped the sweat off my upper lip. Before I entered the house, I turned and spat on the steps near his feet.

"Better watch out real good, boy. You do anything to take that girl away, or even make me think you'll try, she'll be saying 'hello' to your mama up in heaven. If'n that's where she ended up, that is. And after I'm done with ye, that girl'll be next. She looks like a screamer, don't she? How long do ye think she'd be able to stay breathin' if I was good and angry? In my experience they don't last so long once you bring out some farmin' tools. And once their fingernails are all pulled out, they just sorta fall asleep. I keep a bucket of water to revive 'em, but it don't always work. Don't even think about testing me." His threat was the only thing that stopped me from wringing his wrinkled neck.

Opening the door, one thing became clear.

However much my father abhorred his wives and daughters, he hated me more.

# CHRYS

The last letter I got from my cousin said a bunch of stuff about turning sixteen and leaving school. I started to worry that maybe she got swooped up by a husband or something. I pictured her at school—of course it was my high school, which couldn't have been accurate, but it's what I knew—seated at her desk, and a guy on a white stallion entered the classroom.

"Marry me, Rose of Sharon!" he'd say.

She'd drop the notebook and pencil she'd been working with and allow herself to be lifted onto the trusty steed. Then they'd ride away into the sparkling sunset. *Where I would never be able to find her and continue my evil plan of making her want to join us on the dark side.*

Grammy Esther told me that I needed to be more patient, but she wasn't the one living with a dying mother.

Finally, I came home to find the muslin-wrapped Bible on my doorstep. As I approached my front door, Grammy poked her head out of hers, "That man is such a gentleman!

He knocked on my door to make sure that it was safe to leave your package outside. I told him that I was the Neighborhood Watchwoman, and no one dared steal from a stoop in my building. He left the package at your door, but he would not come in for tea. Maybe next time."

It appeared that Mom wasn't the only one who'd been sick. My poor cousin had been recovering from pneumonia.

Here came the guilt again—*wait for it*—I'd been all pissy because she didn't pass me a note. Meanwhile she'd been dying in bed.

I really sucked sometimes.

## JOHN JUNIOR

There was no doubt that my father was not making idle threats. Sadistic behavior was the norm for the wicked man. He had plentiful, loyal friends, wide and deep within the community, who reported often on things that might be of interest to the old man. The only way to protect Catherine was to leave her completely alone.

I just couldn't do it.

Tapping on the bedroom window at Joseph's house, where she was staying until her wedding day, I woke her.

"What is it?" she asked, lifting the window open.

Her hair was tousled from sleep, and she was dressed in a white linen nightdress, flower embroidery stitched along the square collar.

"Get some shoes and come with me, Catherine. I have something I need to tell you."

Hesitating for just the shortest of moments, she pulled on some shoes and then climbed out the window, landing in my arms. She was as light as a child against my chest.

I could have held her like that forever.

Careful to stay in the midnight shadows, I led her to the abandoned barn, laying the blanket that I'd brought across the dirt and pine needles.

There we sat until my voice broke the warm silence.

"I love you, Catherine. Don't tell me there hasn't been enough time, or that I don't know you. There is one thing that I know, and it's that I love you."

She froze, almost imperceptibly leaning away.

"I wanted to marry you. I would have asked you, too, not made you."

"Why are you telling me this, now?" she whispered.

"I just needed you to know. I wanted to warn you that my father..." I choked on my warning, unable to continue.

"What is it?" She grasped my arm, and the warmth soothed me.

"Catherine, I want you to promise me something."

"Okay," she promised, the tiniest glint of fear in her eyes.

"If you ever feel like you're in real danger, you have to leave. Go back to The Outside, and don't return."

"Why don't I just say I changed my mind? Why can't I just cancel the wedding? Maybe I could go with you!"

Her words thrilled me. Just the idea that she would consider being with me was like a salve on my soul.

"It's complicated. Just like my father is complicated. You mustn't try to cancel or ever say my name in front of my father. If you do ... bad things will happen."

"What kind of bad things, John?"

"Trust me, you don't want me to say it. Just promise."

"I promise."

All the air I had been holding in my chest hissed into the night.

"Good. Thank you." I turned to find those entrancing blue eyes searching my face.

"I'll be okay, John. I have to stay with my sister. With her here, everything will be okay."

How I wished that could be true.

*\*\**

On the second night, Catherine was a little surprised that I had returned to her room. But she held my hand as we walked to the barn.

We laughed a lot that night. She told me all about Esther, the eccentric woman who lived across from them in their building. A wise old woman, Esther had acted as a mother to Catherine and Lily. Catherine missed her already.

When we returned to Joseph's house in the wee hours of morning, we shared a kiss. I will never be able to explain in plain words what it was like. God intended for this to happen; there was no other way to explain the way my insides exploded into fire and ice at once. And I could see that she felt it too.

*\*\**

By the third night, she had anticipated my visit. Her

delicately pointed chin resting on her hands, as she looked out into the darkness, grinning when she saw me approach. Without waiting for me to catch her, she climbed onto the windowsill and jumped, landing on the soft soil beneath.

"Hi," she breathed.

I was stunned into silence by the pure, excited energy that waved around her in nearly visible sparks.

Afraid of being caught, she would not speak as we walked. I was even more afraid because I knew what the consequence would have been.

And still, I could not stay away.

When we arrived at the rear of the abandoned barn, she turned to me and grasped both of my hands between hers.

"I want to tell you," she began, boldly, "that I– I love you, too."

At once terrified and overjoyed, sorrow filled me because I knew we could never be together. Exactly ten days remained before the love of my life married my father.

"This is all very tragic, isn't it? We're like Romeo and Juliet, in a way, I suppose." Her words were wistful, hanging in the air around us, drifting up into the trees like melancholy fairies.

We stayed together until morning threatened to reveal us, creeping back as waking lanterns began to flicker within houses all around.

When I joined the delivery crew, I stopped by a bookstore on The Outside. I purchased a copy of *The Great Works of Shakespeare*, reading *Romeo and Juliet* on a couch in the apartment we owned. I continued to read as the delivery team traveled from neighborhood to neighborhood dropping off bundles of the Opus Dei.

Catherine's assessment was accurate. We were star-crossed lovers, just like those she compared us to.

Morbidly, I couldn't help wondering if the end that Romeo and Juliet met was a better one than the future Catherine and I would be forced to endure.

# CHRYS

Grammy had intercepted my delivery from the red-bearded man, but the response folded inside was brief and dissatisfying. Rose of Sharon hadn't returned the Kindle or the iPod, and I couldn't sense any secret message hiding in her writing.

I still needed to write back to her. I scanned the pages in The People's Bible to see if I could make my way through Numbers, because it was the next book my cousin told me to read: *no way*. The words got all weird and floaty when I tried to look at all the...well, all the *numbers*. It was so boring. Why did we need to know who came from who (or *whom*) and how many people lived where?

I thought about loading Wikipedia and taking a look. That's how I was able to write back about the other stuff I was supposed to be learning about. I skimmed the information for Genesis, Exodus, and Leviticus, and then wrote stuff that looked like it might make sense in the border of the book's pages, in pencil.

Honestly, I didn't really care about God's word. I just needed a way to communicate with Rose of Sharon that would make sense to The People. I didn't even feel bad when I cut all those pages up to make room for the Kindle and iPod.

Okay, so maybe I felt a little bit bad.

The last few weeks of school always dragged, but it was worse than ever this year because I was worried about my mom. Every morning she looked like she had aged a decade overnight. She finally couldn't work anymore and was home all the time now.

Large brown spots seemed to magically appear all over the tops of her hands, and every once in a while, she had to lean against a countertop, tabletop, or the back of the couch to catch her breath. Still, she never complained. The doctor gave her some pills for the pain, but they didn't seem to help much.

At school, I pretended to listen to Lauren bluster about what a jerk Steven Ku was, now that he'd dropped her like a hot potato. Sometimes the words just didn't register because I was trying to write a letter in my head. One that would make Rose of Sharon come to us, right away. How could I convey the urgency without alerting other people who might read the letter? I thought about writing a word document or recording my voice and sending it to her, but she still had both devices that would have worked, leaving only the empty carved out space in the big book.

"You are totally not listening to me," Lauren whined.

"You're right," I said, "I'm totally not."

I left her there at the lunch table.

# JOHN JUNIOR

The final week and a half of relative freedom for Catherine erased itself much too quickly. Our nightly meetings became painful because we knew our time together was coming to an end.

"What will my name be, do you suppose?" Catherine wondered.

Most of our women were born into the fold, so the other adults in their families named them, the wives all debating which name suited the infant best.

"Your sister got to choose for herself."

"Yes," Catherine mused, "she has always loved the Lily, so I wasn't surprised."

"What about Iris?" I asked.

"Iris…" She tested the name against her tongue. "Iris – I like it!"

"It was my mother's name," I confessed.

With that, the name *Catherine* was never mentioned again.

***

On the morning of the marriage ceremony, I vomited out in the backyard of my home. I had assured Iris that I would be present among my father, the Elder, and the other wives, while the binding words were said. But by then I started thinking my legs might not be able to hold me while I watched my father steal her away.

My love was dressed in a plain white, shapeless gown when Joseph and Lily brought her to the house. Father took her hand, leading her to the middle of the living room, the wives in a solid circle of resentful unity around them. Joseph and Lily were excused, and they left to sit on the porch and wait.

I cannot say that I recalled even one word of the ceremony. Sweat dripped from every pore. The room swam, and I caught her eye only once. Seeing sadness dull the normally bright blue made me feel as though I might be sick, again. I had a fleeting thought about running away with her, but heard my father talking about farm tools in my mind.

Finally, all the words had been spoken. My heart, no longer beating in my chest for weeks now, but instead in hers, now belonged to my father.

"Well, girl. Ye need a name." Father licked his lips, peering at his newest addition.

"I-I have chosen one, S-Sir," she stammered.

"N-n-n-onsense, girl." He gleefully imitated her

frightened stutter. Then he puffed out his hollow chest and continued, "I'm yer master, now. I get to choose the name I'll be callin' ye. For the rest of yer life." He stretched those last words out, tasting each one behind his rotting teeth.

"Well, Hawkins, tell it, then. We don't have all day, and I need to add the name to the paperwork," the Elder complained.

Father turned toward me, enjoying my pain and overall discomfort, relishing it as one might enjoy a fine meal.

"I got the perfect name," he drawled, about to pull an awful rabbit out of an awful hat. "This here girl is going to take the name of one that was taken from me. She's going to be my replacement. I'm callin' her Iris."

Startled laughter almost erupted from my gut. Iris's eyes swung to me, open wide, a small smile trembling on her lips.

Father thought the name was a kind of punishment, when in actuality it was the perfect wedding gift.

Whenever I heard him speak her name, I would get the thrill of knowing that I had given it to her first.

# CHRYS

"Mom? I have to go to school now, 'kay?" Peeking into her room, I saw her curled up in a ball, an unwatched infomercial flickering across her sleeping face.

Gently sitting on the edge of the bed, I rubbed her back, feeling too many bones beneath the T-shirt she was wearing.

She stirred, asking, "You okay, Chryssy? You doing okay?" Still worried about me, even as she suffered.

"Yeah, Mom, I'm fine. I gotta go to school. Grammy Esther will be by at ten. I'll come home right after, 'kay?"

"Of course, Chrys. Have a wonderful day. Learn a lot and come back to tell me about it."

She had been saying that to me since the first day of kindergarten. Only then, her voice had been much louder and stronger.

\*\*\*

Math crawled. Science crawled. English crawled. Every subject *crawled*; legless zombies dragging themselves across the floor by broken hands. Impatiently, I tapped my pencil on every desk I sat at.

I finally managed to find a way to convey the urgent message that I needed to send to Rose of Sharon. I flipped around that darn Bible, trying to find a quote that fit. I was about to give up when the pages flopped over, like someone else was calling the shots.

And there it was:

Matthew 11:28: "Come unto me, all ye that labour and are heavy laden, and I will give you rest."

I explained in sloppy cursive that this particular passage was *very important to me*. That I wished for her to explain it to me, *as soon as possible,* stressing certain words by underlining them so many times that the paper was ripped away in spots.

Leaving the wrapped-up Bible with Grammy Esther, I instructed her to keep watch for the man with the reddish beard, hoping he would come around in the next few days to see if I needed to deliver a response. *If he doesn't come soon,* I told myself, *I'll go looking for him on the streets again.*

I tried to imagine life without Mom. She explained that Grammy Esther would be my guardian, and I would be allowed to remain living in our apartment. Mom had been gone a lot, working all the time, for most of my life. Even so, the idea of living alone was not welcome *at all.*

I never complained, of course, and held on tight to my plan, knowing that everything would work out if my cousin would just get here in time. I did some research on the internet, trying to find a word for what she was. I had a name for it now.

Necromancer.

# JOHN JUNIOR

My existence became just that. I existed. I felt nothing, tasted nothing. Work became my haven, a mostly unchanging entity filling my days and nights. Orders for the Opus Dei came in on my phone, and I did the paperwork, submitting it for delivery. I had a desk in the blue building, and I would often pass Joseph on the way to it as his office was not far from mine.

We rarely spoke. Having been friends since infancy, not talking to Joseph felt wrong. Like something had ripped the fabric of reality. Any past that we shared was suspended in someone else's history.

We had both lost the women we loved.

When Father spoke the words binding him to Iris, the only way I could function was to pretend she was dead. I avoided the front of the house as much as I could. If we accidentally came face to face, the feelings came smashing into me, taking my breath away. I could tell it was the same for her.

Father monitored us both with hooded eyes, obviously enjoying the agony he inflicted. He was very skilled at causing physical pain, but he was also an expert at mental torture.

I could also sense, without a doubt, that Father had explained the terms of their marriage to Iris: *If I so much as attempted to take her away, she would be killed.*

Soon there was a little girl, a carbon-copy of her mother: big blue eyes and tiny pointed chin, just like Iris's. I should have felt sadness perhaps or have been repulsed by the sight of the baby. But knowing she belonged to my father didn't seem to matter. The child was also a part of Iris, and inexplicably I felt an immovable affection for her. Keeping a safe distance, I watched them together.

The infant seemed to awaken something in her mother. A glow surrounded Iris as she completed her chores with her offspring strapped to her back in a sling. Although I was numb about most everything, the smile that Iris offered her baby let a little bit of warmth crawl back into my core.

The glow left Iris when her sister died.

Lily was due to have a baby very soon after Iris, and she did. The baby lived, but Lily did not survive. Joseph grew darker, and darker, not acknowledging his new daughter. He refused to care for her. For reasons I will never be able to untangle, my father allowed Iris to raise the baby. She rocked and diapered and fed both hers and her sister's during the day, tucked her niece into the crib at night, then returned to the house with the wraparound porch until morning.

Soon Iris's child, named Chrysanthemum by my father's wives, toddled about, followed by Joseph's abandoned child, called Rose of Sharon. I would see them from time to time as I walked past the house on my way to work in the blue building, or as I headed to the bridge to join the delivery crew. They seemed happy.

Iris took her turn picking in the never-ending fields of Opus Dei like every woman in our community, while Joseph's mother volunteered to care for the baby girls. But she really seemed alive only when she was with those children.

Sometimes I would briefly catch Iris's eye. It was almost impossible to look away. On Sundays I would often sit with my father, a row aside and behind her in church, staring at the back of her head. My fingers itching with the remembrance of silken hair being combed between them.

Not long before Chrysanthemum turned two, Iris took her away from The People's Land, escaping under the veil of night, much like we had on our way to the barn, years ago.

Joseph had finally allowed affection for his daughter to enter his heart. Iris must have felt that it was safe to leave her niece, so she had gone.

That night I thanked God for the first time since she was taken from me.

\*\*\*

Many years ticked away. I drifted along with them,

working hard, keeping a schedule. Routine was the only thing that really kept me sane. I tried my hardest not to allow my thoughts to turn toward Iris, but it was often impossible to stop them. Certain she had returned to her apartment on The Outside, I felt a physical pull in that neighborhood's direction every time we visited that part of town for delivery.

Fearing my father's violent hands could still reach her, I never attempted to make contact. If one of my father's goons were to follow me to her door...

***

Joseph and I never rekindled our friendship. He married several more times, bringing many children into the world. I knew he blamed Rose of Sharon for his first wife's death. That poor child became an outcast in the community, her own grandmother declaring her a thing of evil. She had proven to possess a peculiar gift that did not bode well for The People's beliefs. *Only God was allowed to create beautiful things*, it was said. *And only God should have control over life and death.*

I wasn't present the day the field was revived, the dead flowers growing alive in moments; Opus Dei filling the once brown property in a vivid rainbow. It was all the men in the blue building could talk about.

That, and how the child must be of Satan. The Elders went as far as to suggest that the girl should be euthanized, but Joseph insisted that that would be going too far—

probably because the face gazing up at him was a miniscule reminder of his beloved dead wife. He promised to keep her close.

It was a shame to see how she was treated. It tugged at my conscience because it was wrong, but also because she looked so much like her mother. And Iris.

They were Iris's eyes that looked up at me in that girl's face on that dark morning.

When Rose of Sharon approached with that package, saying that her father had authorized the transaction, I felt something shift within me. My father felt it also and studied me as I accepted the package. It was as if he was challenging me to make a move.

And if I made the wrong one, Iris's life could be in danger.

# CHRYS

E ven though I wanted to spend every possible moment
away from school with my mom, I couldn't resist
joining Lauren for a soft serve on the way home.

Since she wasn't with Steven anymore, she'd lost her
transportation and was forced to hoof it along with the rest
of us poor, carless souls.

"I'm sorry I acted so pissy," Lauren apologized. "I
know your mom is really sick. I shouldn't expect you to be
thinking about anything else but that. Sometimes I just
forget."

I forgave her when she offered to pay for my treat.

The stop at Foster's Freeze took maybe ten minutes.
I've never wished for ten minutes to be returned to me so
badly.

I sensed that something was wrong the second I
opened the door to our building. Everything was way too
still. No classical music leaked from Grammy's apartment,
as it always did.

And there was a note on our door, in shaky arthritic scrawl:

*Chrys,*
*Come to the hospital, quick.*
*Your mom has been rushed there.*
*Don't dawdle,*
*Grammy Esther*

Barely able to fit my key in our lock with my shaking hands, I swung the door open just enough to throw my backpack inside.

The hospital was just under two miles from our house, and I sprinted the entire way. Reaching the information desk, I bent at the waist, struggling to catch my breath.

"Catherine Perkins, please," I panted.

I was directed to the fourth floor, and then led to a private room by a nurse at the reception desk on that floor.

Mom looked tiny on that hospital bed. The covers were pulled up to her chin, eyes closed. I ran to her side.

"Mom!" I whispered, horrified I might not have made it in time.

Her eyes opened, and she turned her head toward me.

"I'm okay, Chrys. I'm okay, I swear."

*Whatever.* The woman lying in front of me did *not* look okay.

"They wanted to hook her up to those machines, but she wouldn't let them," a low voice to my right said.

The man who had picked up and dropped off packages

for Rose of Sharon and me sat in an orange plastic chair.

"This is John," introduced Grammy Esther. "He found Cathy and called an ambulance."

I hadn't even noticed her there.

"I came to see if you had another letter for me. I knocked on the door, but no one answered. It was unlocked, so I went inside and found her. She was on the floor."

"He came to my apartment," began Grammy, "and woke me up. I had fallen asleep watching my stories. He rode in the ambulance, but I called a taxi."

"Okay, well, you can go now." Looking at the man before me, I willed him to leave my family in peace.

"No," from the hospital bed came a soft voice.

"Mom, I want to talk to you about your options, again. You're just lying there *doing nothing*! You're not trying to save yourself *at all*! I hate this!" I dissolved into angry tears, "I hate this!"

"Listen to me, Chrysanthemum. This is how it's supposed to be." Tears fell from her eyes now, too. I felt like a jerk, as usual.

*"But you're leaving me all alone."*

"You won't be alone, Honey. You'll have Grammy Esther. And you'll have John."

Swinging to glare at the man in the weird clothes, the weird hat, and the weird beard, I returned my stare to my mother.

"What do you mean, Mother? *'And you'll have John.'* What is that?!* He's just a guy from that cuckoo cult!" I knew I should try to be calm and patient with her, and that her brain might not be functioning as well as it used to. I was just too frustrated, and afraid of losing my mother.

"He's not just a guy from The People's Land, Chrys," her breath was too shallow. She struggled to produce her speech, "he's your father."

John jumped to his feet, and our eyes connected, mouths agape. In unison we turned to look at my mom.

John approached the bed, kneeling at Mom's side, gently grasping her hand.

"Why didn't you tell me, Catherine. Why? All that time..."

"What difference would it have made, John? Would it have been any easier for you? No, it would have been so much harder. And now look, there's nothing more your father can do to me." A sly smile crept across her greying face.

"You can't go, now, Catherine. Please don't go," he begged.

"...so tired..." She closed her eyes, drifting off into sleep, her chest struggling to rise and fall as she breathed.

The man on the floor looked up at me.

"I have always loved her. *She's the only one I've ever loved.*"

"Well, if you really love her, then you know what you have to do."

"Yes," he agreed, standing, "I'll return as quickly as I can."

And before I could come up with some awkward quip

about fathers and daughters thinking alike, he was already gone.

# JOHN JUNIOR

I wasn't terribly concerned about what the delivery team thought of my absence that afternoon. Although it wasn't a regular occurrence for me, it wasn't unusual for one or more of the men to spend extra time on The Outside with a lady friend or holed up in the apartment until the crew arrived again in the morning. I just hoped the bright yellow car I hired to bring me back didn't alarm anyone. Most likely no one would be anywhere near the bridge this late, but it is in my nature to worry. There have been too many coincidences in my life not to.

Pulling my key ring out of my rear pocket, I unlocked the double lock on the gate and entered The People's Land. The cabbie counted his money, waving as he drove off.

Hurrying to Joseph's house, I crept out to the back of the property, approaching Rose of Sharon's room. No light reached around the cracks, so I thought she must be sleeping. When I opened the door, I heard a squeal.

A little girl rolled under the bed, looking up at me with

fear.

"Who are you?" I asked in surprise. As far as I knew, no one was allowed in this room but its owner.

"I'm Wee Lilac," she said slowly, her mouth working around an absence of teeth.

"Where's Rose of Sharon?"

"I didn't mean anything by it, honest. I just miss her." A cat meowed in agreement, from somewhere behind the child, who pulled herself out and up.

"Where's Rose of Sharon?" I repeated, feeling the moments slip through my fingers.

"Father sent her to live with the mean man. She's supposed to marry him in the morning." Wee Lilac lifted the cat to her shoulders.

"When you say, 'the mean man,' do you mean John Senior?" My mouth became impossibly dry.

"Yeah, he's the one. He beats 'em all, the kids at school say. Freckled Peony had a black eye last week, and-"

I cut her off. She wasn't telling me anything I didn't already know.

"Thank you, Lilac."

***

*This can't possibly be happening again,* I mused, almost entertained by the bizarreness of it all. *It's like my father has made an ugly goal of gathering up females who are important to me and stealing them away.*

Instinct told me that he would stop at nothing to keep me away from his betrothed. I was on very dangerous ground.

Most of the wives and children had already gone to bed. Two women still toiled in the kitchen, washing dishes. I crept around to the back of the house, wondering where my father could be. My answer came swiftly: He walked out of the back bushes, pulling up his zipper, a cigar between his teeth.

His off-key humming told me that he'd been into his whiskey. The People aren't supposed to imbibe alcohol, but like so many rules of our community, the men chose which ones to adhere to, however they pleased.

Pressing my back against the wall, I stepped into the vegetable garden and watched warily as he turned the corner. He would be headed to the front porch, I knew. In his state, he would probably end up sleeping there, leaning against the railing.

*How could this have happened?* I went over it again in my mind.

Father had always been great at pulling strings. However, there was still the mystery of how I had missed this new engagement altogether. Something must have happened that made Joseph desperate. I rarely paid attention to anything happening in the community. Lately I was so depressed about losing Young Luke that I retired to the blue building to work in my office, unable to bear the wails of his mother and everyone else who loved him.

I felt like I could enter the house without anyone

seeing me this time of the evening, so I slipped into the back door, able to hear the women still working in the kitchen. Creeping down the long dark hallway, I finally came to the office door. It was locked.

When I entered the room, Rose of Sharon jumped and hid something behind her back.

"It's you!" she exclaimed.

"Yes."

"Not him."

"We have to leave. Quickly, Rose of Sharon. If we don't go now, I'll never be able to get you out of here. Just leave your things, and let's move!" I whispered with urgency.

"I can't leave my things. Some of them belong to my cousin."

It seemed that she decided to trust me. She held up two electronic devices to show me, then stuffed them in her bag, slinging it across her chest.

I closed the door behind us to buy us some more time in case someone walked down the hall. An open door would have raised the alarm. We crept along the back of the house, and I almost felt the wonderful relief of freedom.

"What do ye think yer doin', John Junior?" My father stepped around from the front of the house, his face twisted in malice.

"Run!" I yelled at my rescuee, ready to sprint—but not sure where.

I watched the girl fly out before me, but I was being held back. My father had a grip on the back of my trousers.

There was a ripping noise, and then I flew along to meet Rose of Sharon.

"I can't catch up to ye," I heard called out into the night, "but I'll get ye. Just you wait!"

"Follow me," Joseph's daughter pulled me down a familiar path.

When we reached the back of the abandoned barn, she stopped.

"I think we'll be safe here. At least for a little while," she explained, out of breath.

"I've been here before," I said. Dozens of happy memories flew at me, like a person seeing his life flash before his eyes. *These memories were my life.* The only part of it that mattered.

Rose of Sharon looked like she maybe had a few memories of her own. She stared ahead, but I couldn't see what she was seeing; she, too, was lost in thought.

"Do you think Peter will hear about what happened?" she asked, dreamily. "I hope he doesn't worry too much. He's always so worried."

"We need to get to the bridge soon," I explained, "Father won't waste much time sending his friends after us."

"Let's go now," she said, snapping out of her reverie. "I can make it. I needed to catch my breath, but I think I'm all right now."

"There's something I need to do. It won't take but a moment. Wait for me here."

I left her there, nervous about leaving her alone. When

I returned a while later, she still stood where she had before.

"Now we're going to have to run," I urged. "Run for your life, Shar'n."

We reached the bridge in no time. I was impressed with the girl's endurance, as she remained with me, neck and neck, the entire way. Our feet made familiar hollow noises on the bridge. I reached into my pocket to pull out the keys.

But the entire pocket was gone, torn away. It was the one my father had held me by.

"Listen to me, Rose of Sharon." I grasped her arms so she would focus on my face. "We're going to have to swim. It's going to be cold. And rough. But we're going to have to do it."

"I've never swam before." She looked more distressed than she had all night.

"This will be your first lesson," I said. I grabbed her bag, then mine, tossing them across the river. Mine reached the shore, the strap catching on a low-hanging branch. Hers missed altogether, and she watched in horror as it rushed away from us, caught in the river's flow.

"I have to-" She began to enter the water in the direction of the quickly receding satchel.

"Just leave it. Believe me, it's going to be okay."

Pulling her waist-deep into the freezing water, I held onto her arm with one hand and a large boulder with the other. The water would soon be up to our eyes, and then our feet wouldn't touch at all. The current was strong enough to carry a large man away, let alone someone Rose of Sharon's size.

"Okay," I spoke up, my words barely audible above the rushing water, "you're going to have to hold your breath in a bit. Don't be afraid, just hold on."

Icy wet covered us, shocking us both. She gripped my arm with her hands, her fingernails digging into my nearly numb skin. The current was powerful and it pulled me toward the bridge. I could see men standing there now guarding the gate.

Kicking with all the strength I could muster, I dragged my precious cargo along, coming up so every few seconds so we could breathe. After what seemed like frigid hours, we reached a spot where my feet found purchase in the claylike surface. Standing on the bank we tried to catch our breath.

"See those men over there?" I asked her, pointing in the direction of the bridge. My hand shook vigorously. "They think they're waiting for us so stay down. We're going to head in the other direction. Keep low."

She nodded, her cheeks quivering with cold.

Looping my bag around my shoulder, I pulled my partner in crime toward a lone, thick pine tree, giving us a moment to breathe.

"When I say, 'Go,' I want you to run as fast as you can. If we can get a bit further before they see us, we might be able to make it. Once we get to the city's border we'll be safe."

Looking up at me with those huge eyes, hair dripping,

shivering in the breeze, I wondered why I hadn't gotten her out sooner. All those years I watched her suffer humiliation and isolation. I knew she had family on The Outside yet I'd done nothing to reunite them.

Now was my chance. I would not fail.

"Okay," I warned her. "Go!"

Through the low brush, rocks, and powdery dirt, we sped. With virtually nowhere to hide, there was no choice but to make it to the border.

"Come on, come on, come on!" I urged when she began to slow.

Although I knew we were getting closer, the yards seemed to multiply in front of us, never ending. The voices I had been dreading echoed in the distance, shouting in alarm.

*It will take them a while to unlock that gate in this dark and we've made it about three quarters of a mile so there's at least ten minutes between us,* I calculated.

"Almost there!" My chest and legs burned. My muscles were so cold from the water that they couldn't quite function properly. Streetlights stretched out in front of us, a neighborhood just a block away.

This time, it was Rose of Sharon doing the pushing.

"I can hear them! Move it! *Faster!*" Arms and legs pumping wildly, she pulled in front of me for the last stretch.

We arrived in front of a row of houses with expansive front yards, farm-style homes on the outskirts of The Outside.

"Don't stop, yet. Around the corner, come on!"

Finally, out of sight we stopped, gasping for breath. Rose of Sharon looked around, still not sure of our safety.

"We're all right now," I assured her. "But we've got a way to go. Can you walk?"

Still not recovered from the exertion, she put her hands on her hips, walking in circles. But she nodded her head. She would continue.

"Why did you save me?" she asked.

The few people on the street gave us curious looks. I couldn't imagine what they thought of the strangely dressed couple dripping in the moonlight.

"Your cousin asked me to fetch you. She needs your help."

"How could I possibly help her? She lives out here, with all this technology and free knowledge. Whatever problem she has, she could read a book or hop on the internet – and *problem solved.* I have nothing to offer."

*How did this girl know so much of the world?*

"Not true, child. Think about it. There is one thing that only you can do."

"I didn't think she knew about that. I thought she'd stop writing if she knew…" Rose of Sharon slowed a bit, shaking her head in wonder.

"You'll understand when we get to the hospital."

# CHRYS

W hen they entered the room, Grammy Esther gasped. Rose of Sharon could have been my twin, or at least a nearly identical sister. In really weird, very wet clothes.

"Lily is that you?" a frail voice called excitedly from the far side of the room.

My cousin approached the hospital bed, looking down at my mother.

"I knew you would come for me, Lily. I've missed you so, so much."

"Mom," I stepped in, "this isn't Lily. This is Rose of Sharon."

"Oh!" Tears trickled down Mom's cheeks, running sideways onto her pillow. "Rose of Sharon, I'm so sorry we left you behind. We had to get out, and your mother—and there was your father to think of..."

"Please don't cry," the girl said. "I remember so many of the good things that you did for me. You were the only one who ever really made me feel loved."

And now we were *all* crying.

Rose of Sharon took mother's hands and leaned forward, kissing her on the forehead.

She said, "I'm here to help you. It won't be long now. I'll bring you back, and whatever has made you ill will be gone. I promise it won't hurt you at all."

Turning toward me, she smiled. It was my mother's smile – right down to the left canine hanging just the tiniest bit lower than the right.

Grammy Esther walked up next to me and whispered, "I knew she would make it in time."

"How did you know?" I asked, in disbelief.

"If you'd ever finished reading *The Grapes of Wrath* like you're supposed to, you'd see that the character, Rose of Sharon, is the only one with any hope left in the end. And she is also a giver of life."

*I made a mental note to finish reading that damn book, even if it killed me.*

# JOHN JUNIOR

L ooking down at the woman I had adored for almost half of my life, seeing her almost gone from this world, the fiery, unrelenting Hell the Host Elder preached in church on Sundays couldn't hold a candle to this brand of torture.

"Oh, John," she breathed, "I'm so glad you know now. So glad."

"But we can be a family now, Iris, just let Rose of–" I begged, but she interrupted.

"Your father would never allow that, John."

Breathing deep, she looked at us all surrounding her.

"Everyone in the world that I love, all here together," she sighed, as her eyes closed.

And she was gone.

Before I could tell her about our insurance policy.

# CATHERINE

I changed my mind.
I thought I knew what I wanted, what was right. But I changed my mind anyway.

Seeing all those beloved faces circling me, I finally felt at peace. For so many years I worried about how things would reach a resolution, and it was a happy ending to our very difficult story. They had all been brought together – by God, I had no doubt – and they would take care of each other.

*This is how it's supposed to be*, I confidently thought.

Feeling as though I was cradled in a pair of great hands, rocking me smoothly side to side, I saw an angel.

I couldn't see her with my eyes, but I felt her everywhere – even inside of me. Her voice was heartbreakingly familiar.

*Lily.*

"It's not time to go yet, Cathy. You have to let her do it. Please let her do it. This story is not over just yet."

It was almost impossible to find air, and my eyes wouldn't open however hard I tried, but *I clawed my way back.* Away from the brilliant light and the wonderful caress, I crawled. Heaving, I found my way back to that hospital.

"Do it," I gasped.

# EPILOGUE

S o, this is *Happy Ever After.*

Learning how to use a microwave took some practice, and sometimes I worried that taking selfies would steal my soul—but only because I took so many of them. I loved TV, too, and was amazed by the behavior of people all over the world. I was dazzled by the grocery store and couldn't eat enough McNuggets on a recent lunch outing. The sights, smells, and sounds of The Outside were completely overwhelming in the most wonderful way.

Daily, Aunt Cathy hugged me, whispering, "Thank you, dear Fleur, thank you, thank you."

The events of the night of her almost-demise will never completely fade away, I fear.

When she said those last words, giving me permission to bring her back, I rushed to her side, pushing everyone out of the way. As soon as I was sure she was really gone, I began my work.

Placing my hands on her emaciated chest, I felt the fizz

in my fingertips almost immediately, because she had been gone for mere seconds. As it never had with animals or insects, the vibrations reached my elbows, my shoulders, taking over my entire body in violent aftershocks, once the process was complete.

I didn't feel any different than usual, other than being overly drained. But I knew, without a doubt, that my gift had vanished.

The minutes following the miracle became a chaotic whirlwind of activity. Grammy Esther transformed into a drill sergeant, barking orders at everyone in the room:

"Chrys, go tell the nurses your mother wants to return home to die in peace."

"Cathy, for God sakes, stop looking so damn alive."

"John, gather your things and call a taxi."

"Rose of Sharon, come sit down, dear. You look like you might vomit."

The nurses came to the room, saying that Catherine's doctor didn't think anything more could be done for her anyway, since she refused any sort of medical care, and had even signed a DNR form. Once the cab arrived, they wheeled her out and helped her inside. John sat next to her.

"We'll call another one," assured Grammy, barely holding me up.

***

It turned out that the Opus Dei was anything *but* God's Work, as its name insinuated. The genus was created by a group of scientists who worked tirelessly in the blue building, developing a species with a head the size of a smaller dinner plate in a variety of unnaturally bright colors that had the ability to grow within a matter of days. It wasn't the soil that was special; It was genetic engineering. By splicing irradiated bacteria DNA into the genome of the flowers, the scientists produced seeds that grew flowers of incredible size and color variation. They were safe enough where they were, isolated from the rest of the world, but cross-pollinate them with flowers on The Outside—and no one knew what would happen, not even the scientists in the blue building.

And John had the documents to prove it.

"Imagine what will happen to The People," John said, "if every flower-buying business on The Outside finds out that the holy Opus Dei is nothing but a fraud, and a dangerous one at that? They would be done within hours."

He explained that, while his father was a vindictive man who would quite possibly dare to visit them to exact some sort of revenge, the knowledge that John Junior held in his little white plastic binder kept them all safe. Any action that John Senior might attempt would lead to the revelation of the origins of the Opus Dei, and the old man knew he wouldn't survive long in The People's Land if he was responsible for the fall of their empire.

Practically my entire life was a string of strange events, but the strangest of them all was that it had been *my father* who gave the documents to John Junior. He even made the copies himself. When John left me behind the barn during our escape, he had hoped to enter the blue building to find something that would help us. He didn't expect anyone to be there, but my father was working late. Maybe Dark Joseph was a bit less dark than I'd always thought. He also sent a gift for me, and it arrived in John Junior's bag; the little wooden box that I'd borrowed from behind Father's encyclopedias, once, long ago. The baby blanket with my name stitched on it was inside, along with the note from my mother. The sketch of her likeness, however, was gone.

I believed this meant that my father had held some love for me all along, maybe even just a little. Although it could have just as easily been that he wanted to honor the memory of his first wife. I'll never know, but I decided that was okay.

Like my aunt, I was a true fan of irony. We laughed over the fact that I had spent my whole life yearning for a family who would accept me despite my gift, and when I'd found one who loved me *because* of it (in part, at least), the gift was gone, forever.

When I laid in my bed wide awake listening to the sound of Chrys breathing on the other side of our room, I couldn't help but wonder what would have happened if I had managed to bring Young Luke back, or if John Junior hadn't rescued me in time and I'd resurrected his father. Would I have possessed enough power to raise my aunt?

I've settled on a theory, but I am glad I won't ever have to test it.

\*\*\*

Uncle John secured a job at a nearby flower shop almost instantly. His business prowess in the field was well-known on a local scale. They gave him a managerial position—with a promise that they would never place an order for the Opus Dei, or any other product, with The People's Land. They gladly accepted his terms.

Officially enrolled at Chrys's school, Ritter High, I was a couple months away from becoming a Sophomore, just one year behind Chrys. I had a lot to learn about science, math, history—pretty much every subject except for English and maybe home economics. The school district was aware of Aunt Cathy's tutoring skills, though, and everyone had high hopes for me. Even me. I decided that I want to be a writer, like my aunt. I had quite a story to tell, and school is the best way to start, although no one would ever believe it to be true, so it might be labeled as fiction.

Summer days were spent at the neighborhood pool with Chrys and Lauren, and a few dozen other people in a near-naked state. The sight of my own bare legs startled me for quite a while, but I learned to swim, which was exhilarating. Everyone called me Fleur. Even though Lauren and most of Chrys's other friends wanted to know why someone with a name like "Floor" wouldn't pick "like, a nickname or something". I sort of enjoyed explaining the meaning behind the name my mother chose for me.

The only thing missing wasn't a thing at all, but rather

a "he."

My nightmares were filled with Peter and a selection of wives, proudly watching fields filled with skinny, freckled, wild-haired children running about. I prayed that his father was being kind enough, and although Uncle John warned us all to stay as far away from the black delivery buggies as we could, I couldn't help but linger for a few seconds hoping to catch sight of him.

***

Chrys and I entered our apartment building after a day of sunshine and swimming. My wet towel was wrapped around my neck, and pool water soaked through my clothing from my bathing suit beneath.

"You!" Grammy Esther pointed at me, waving me into her apartment. Chrys shrugged and moved to our own front door.

Grammy began speaking even before I entered her front room.

"This boy will be renting a room from me. He needs a place to stay. I have an extra bedroom and I need help around this place."

"Hi, Fleur," he said. The blue jeans and black hoodie were all wrong; in my dreams, awake and asleep, he wore a straw hat, suspenders—and black pants just a couple of inches short for his lanky form.

Approaching me with a crooked grin, Peter said, "I just got back from enrolling for my senior year at Ritter High. I figured you might want some company at the lunch table."

# ABOUT THE AUTHOR

Shauna McGuiness is a reluctant California Girl who would choose rain over sunshine any day. She lives with her high school sweetheart, two children, and Shih Tzu, Bravo.